# Sleeping Beauty

Kaye Umansky

Illustrated by Caroline Crossland

A & C BLACK • LONDON

# *Contents*

# A Letter from the Playwright

I decided to adapt the story of Sleeping Beauty for two reasons. Firstly, it's such a popular, well-loved tale, full of romance and lashings of drama. Secondly, it has a large number of characters – an important consideration when one is looking for a play which will involve a great many children.

I have no way of knowing how many children will be involved in your production. I have attempted to make the play flexible enough to perform with a single class or small drama group or, alternatively, a mighty whole-school project involving each and every child in some capacity – either as actors, dancers, members of the choir or orchestra, members of the stage management team or designers of scenery, costumes, props and programmes.

There are twenty-two speaking parts in the play: fifteen female, seven male. (The preponderance of females is as a result of the thirteen Fairies). The parts of Nursey and Prince Valentine can be played by either sex. There are, however, plenty of non-speaking parts which would be suitable for boys, i.e. The Kitchen Staff, the Guards and the Gardeners. I have purposely left the numbers vague. If you are working with a limited number of children, two of each would suffice. You can, however, have as many as you can comfortably fit into your acting area.

Extra parts have been created if you need to swell the cast to accommodate vast numbers of children, i.e. The Villagers and the Spiders. The Villagers appear twice – in the Prologue and Act 1, Scene 4. In the Prologue, they sing a short song. If you wish, you could extend this scene to include a country dance. In Scene 4, they speak in chorus. If you need even more extra parts, children could play trees in the forest scenes.

If, on the other hand, you are not looking to extend your cast, the Villagers can be excluded. Both scenes can be adapted so that the Town Crier addresses the audience directly. In the Prologue, the audience and off-stage cast can perform the cheers and the song can be omitted. Nightshade's speech at the end of Scene 4 can be easily modified as follows:

NIGHTSHADE: So, you think that'll make a difference? Well, it won't! A curse is a curse and it'll take more that a stupid royal decree to lift it!

As for the Spiders, you can have as few as three or accommodate an entire infant class, if you wish.

With regard to the speaking parts, there are six characters with large roles. These are: King Bertie, Queen Betty, Nursey, the Lord Chamberlain, the Town Crier and Nightshade. There are fourteen medium-sized roles: the twelve Fairies, Beauty and Prince Valentine. There are two small roles: The Cook and The Footman. The latter only says one line, but provides a good deal of comic relief. (Talking of comedy, when the children are rehearsing, do point out that they will need to pause to allow time for audience laughter when they have delivered a funny line.)

Do feel free to adapt this play to suit your needs. The script is not set in stone. Cut things out, add extra jokes with topical references to the school or locality, put in additional songs or dances. Above all, have fun with it.

Break a leg!

# Characters In Order Of Appearance

The Twelve Good Fairies:
    Bluebell
    Primrose
    Snowdrop
    Holly
    Marigold
    Poppy
    Daffodil
    Lilac
    Rose
    Iris
    Willow
    Violet
    Nightshade – the thirteenth
      fairy

The Town Crier
King Bertie
Queen Betty
The Footman
The Lord Chamberlain
Nursey
The Cook
The Kitchen Staff
The Guards
The Gardeners
Princess Beauty
The Spiders
Prince Valentine

# List of Scenes and their Locations

| | | |
|---|---|---|
| Prologue Part 1 – | Fairy Talk | The Forest |
| Prologue Part 2 – | Great News! | The Crossroads |

Act 1
| | | |
|---|---|---|
| Scene 1 – | Our Baby | The Castle Throne Room |
| Scene 2 – | Invitations | The Forest |
| Scene 3 – | The Christening | The Castle Throne Room |
| Scene 4 – | Bad News! | The Crossroads |

(Interval if desired)

Act 2
| | | |
|---|---|---|
| Scene 1 – | Birthday Preparations | The Castle Kitchen |
| Scene 2 – | The Curse | The Tower Room |
| Scene 3 – | Time Passes | The Castle Kitchen |
| Scene 4 – | Prince Valentine | The Forest |
| Scene 5 – | The Happy Ending | The Castle Kitchen/ Tower Room |

# Prologue – Part 1 – Fairy Talk

*The Forest. Moonlight. In the background, the towers of a distant castle can be seen rising above the trees. As the musical introduction to the first song begins, the lights come up to reveal twelve FAIRIES standing in a ring.*

TWELVE LITTLE FAIRIES
*(The Fairies sing and dance to the tune of 'In A Cottage In A Wood')*

1. In the middle of the wood,
   Twelve Little Fairies, sweet and good
   Dance around a fairy ring
   Beneath a harvest moon,
   What a charming start, you say,
   This will be a lovely play,
   Twelve Little Fairies dancing round
   To such a pretty tune.

2. Are you comfy in your seat?
   You're in for a lovely treat,
   Settle back and watch us as we
   Point our tiny toes...

*(Thunder, flashing lights. The song ends in chaos as the startled Fairies scream and scatter. Enter NIGHTSHADE, the thirteenth fairy.)*

| | |
|---|---|
| NIGHTSHADE: | Enough! No more, d'you hear? Any more of that racket and I'll come and kick your stupid fairy ring down. *(To Audience)* Shall I? *(Pause for Audience response.)* Ah, you're as cissy as that lot. |
| BLUEBELL: | That is sooo typical of you, Nightshade. Always spoiling things when we're having a good time. |
| PRIMROSE: | Trying to scare us with your threats. Anyway, you can't kick our ring down. It's built of Good Magic. |

*(They re-group, forming a ring. They raise their wands and shake them, NIGHTSHADE hisses and draws back.)*

| | |
|---|---|
| SNOWDROP: | Good Magic is stronger than bad. |
| NIGHTSHADE: | Hah! So says you. |
| HOLLY: | Want to put it to the test? Try stepping into the Ring. |
| NIGHTSHADE: | Not tonight, thank you. |
| MARIGOLD: | You see? You can't. |

NIGHTSHADE: Oh yes I can.

ALL: Oh no you can't!

NIGHTSHADE: Oh, yes I can!

ALL: Oh no you can't.

NIGHTSHADE: I can! I can if I want to! I just can't be bothered to play your pathetic little games.

(the FAIRIES come out of their circle and stand at ease.)

POPPY: Why are you so mean and horrible, Nightshade?

DAFFODIL: D'you know what I think? I think it's because you're jealous. You want to be a member of our Fairy Club.

NIGHTSHADE: Me? Jealous of your soppy club? Where you dance on tippy toes and get Brownie Points for being good?

LILAC: What's wrong with being good? You should try it some time.

NIGHTSHADE: I'd sooner swim with sharks.

ROSE: Oh, come on, give it a go. Join our club. We don't just dance and sing.

IRIS: We weave spells that help people along a little.

WILLOW: We grant wishes and reward good deeds.

(Everyone looks expectantly at VIOLET, who has yet to speak.)

FAIRIES: Go on, Violet. Your turn.

(VIOLET takes a deep breath, then goes all shy.)

FAIRIES: (to audience) She's shy.

NIGHTSHADE: I've never heard of anything so revolting in my life. Look at you! You're so smug! (To Audience) Aren't they smug? Ah, why am I asking you? They're smug all right. Now, me, I like to live dangerously. Stir things up a little. Who needs to join a cissy club for goody-goodies when you can have loads more fun making trouble!

NIGHTSHADE'S FIRST SONG
*(NIGHTSHADE sings, to the tune of 'God Rest Ye Merry Gentlemen')*

1.    I am a trouble maker,
It's plain for all to see,
It's something that's developed
In my personality,
If ever things need stirring up,
Don't hesitate, call me,
I will give you an estimate for free,
Totally free,
I will give you an estimate for free.

2.    I specialise in misery
Disaster and dismay,
If you should try to cross me,
I'll make sure that you will pay,
I'll give you crops of pimples
I'll make your hair turn grey
I can spoil happy endings in a play,
Have a bad day,
I can spoil happy endings in a play!

Just watch me! Ha ha ha ha ha *(Screaming with wicked laughter, NIGHTSHADE exits, to thunder.)*

BLUEBELL:    Well, thank goodness she's gone. Now we can get on with the main business of the night. The Spell!

ALL:    Yes! Yes! Let's do The Spell!

PRIMROSE:    Into the circle.

SNOWDROP:    Wands up!

*(They form a circle with their wands raised.)*

ALL:    In yonder palace sits a queen.
She weeps upon the throne.
And wishes for her heart's desire –
A baby of her own.
She has no use for diamonds
She has no use for gold.
She simply wants a baby
To rock and love and hold.
Wind and waves and fire and water
Give our queen a baby daughter!

*(Lights down. Exit FAIRIES.)*

# Prologue – Part 2 – Great News!

*In the darkness, there is the sound of church bells pealing in celebration. Lights up on The Crossroads. Enter the TOWN CRIER, ringing his bell. He stands by a signpost. Three arms point "To The Forest", "To The Castle" and "To The Village". The VILLAGERS enter and gather around him.*

| | |
|---|---|
| TOWN CRIER: | Oyez! Oyez! Great news! Know that this day, Her Most Royal Majesty, Queen Bettina, is delivered of a baby daughter. Name, yet to be chosen. Weight, seven pounds. His Majesty King Bertrand declares this day a national holiday in celebration. Three cheers for the proud parents. Hip hip… |
| VILLAGERS: | Hooray! |

A BABY GIRL IS BORN TODAY
*(TOWN CRIER and VILLAGERS sing to the tune of 'The Animals Went in Two by Two')*

> A baby girl is born today, hooray! Hooray!
> A baby girl is born today, hooray! Hooray!
> We're ever so pleased, we're ever so glad,
> Good wishes go to her mum and her dad,
> Let us raise the roof, a baby is born today. Hooray!

*(Exit TOWN CRIER and VILLAGERS.)*

# Act 1, Scene 1 – Our Baby

*The Castle Throne Room. QUEEN BETTY and KING BERTIE are sitting on their thrones, gazing into a heavily beribboned crib. They are both clearly besotted. A bored looking FOOTMAN stands in the background, his arms piled high with cuddly toys and rattles. KING BERTIE is tickling the unseen baby with a feather and making nauseating baby talk while the QUEEN looks fondly on.*

| | |
|---|---|
| KING BERTIE: | Tiddly iddly iddly. Tiddly iddly. Oo's Daddy's ickle precious? Look! Look at that! She smiled, see? *(excitedly, to the FOOTMAN, who looks blank.)* She smiled! She smiled! |
| QUEEN BETTY: | Ahhhhh. |
| KING BERTIE: | Boodly oodly. Diddly widdly. *(He snaps his fingers at the Footman.)* Duck. Quickly, man, quickly! |

*(The FOOTMAN places a rubber duck in the KING's hand, in the manner of a nurse passing an instrument to a surgeon.)*

KING BERTIE: Who's dis? It's Mr Ducky Wucky. Quack! Quack! Quaaaaack! Look! She did it again, Betty!

KING/QUEEN: Aaaaaaah. Our baby.

KING BERTIE: *(to FOOTMAN)* Rattle. No, make that the pink rabbit.

*(The FOOTMAN passes the KING the rabbit.)*

KING BERTIE: Whoooooo's dis? It's Mr Floppetty Woppitty bunnikins. Ooooh yes it is. Ooooh yes it is.

QUEEN BETTY: We ought to be thinking of a name for her, you know, darling. Any ideas?

KING BERTIE: Well, you know, I've been thinking about that. I'm Bertie and you're Betty. I think she should have a name that sounds a bit similar, don't you?

QUEEN BETTY: What – Batty or something?

KING BERTIE: Well, perhaps not Batty. Batty, Betty, Bitty, Botty. *(to the baby)* What shall we call you, eh? Is oo daddy's little Botty? Is oo? *(to the FOOTMAN)* Rattle! *(the FOOTMAN tiredly passes the rattle.)* Does oo like oo's rattle wattle? Does oo? *(There is a knock. Enter the LORD CHAMBERLAIN. He bows to the royal couple.)*

KING BERTIE: *(still talking baby-speak)* And whoooooo's dis?

LORD CHAM: The Lord Chamberlain-Wamberlain, sire. Begging a moment of your royal time.

KING BERTIE: *(recovering)* Ahem. Of course, Lord Chamberlain. Come in, come in. Getting a bit carried away there, you know? First time dad and all that.

LORD CHAM: Of course, sire, quite understandable. It's just that the applicant for the Nurse's job is waiting outside.

QUEEN BETTY Applicant? Only the one? I thought you said there were quite a few?

| | |
|---|---|
| LORD CHAM: | Well, there were to start with, but I think this one's frightened the rest away, ma'am. |
| QUEEN BETTY: | Frightened? How do you mean, frightened? Was it her manner or something? |
| LORD CHAM: | More likely her wig, ma'am. And the nasty way she has with her thermometer. |
| QUEEN BETTY: | Oh. Well, I suppose you'd better bring her in. |
| KING BERTIE: | By the way, Lord Chamberlain. What d'you think of Botty as a name? |
| LORD CHAM: | Princess Botty. Hmm. I'll have to think about that one, sire. |

*(The LORD CHAMBERLAIN exits.)*

| | |
|---|---|
| KING BERTIE: | Are you quite sure about this, darling? Do we really need a nurse? Are we doing the right thing? |
| QUEEN BETTY: | I think so, darling. It's a royal sort of thing to do, isn't it? |
| KING BERTIE: | But babies need their mummies and daddies. |
| QUEEN BETTY: | It's not you who gets up in the middle of the night, though, is it, darling? Sssh. Here she comes. |

*(Enter the LORD CHAMBERLAIN, followed by NURSEY. She wears traditional nurses uniform teamed with a huge, ginger wig, big boots and stripy tights. Scissors, watch and thermometer protrude from her capacious apron pocket.)*

| | |
|---|---|
| LORD CHAM: | Your Majesties – may I present – er – ahem – Nursey. |
| NURSEY: | Where is she? Where's my little angel? Aha! *(She strides to the crib.)* Oooh, look at that! Fast asleep. There's a good little baby. Nursey will give you a lovely bathikins when you wake up. |
| KING BERTIE: | Er – one moment, my good woman. You haven't got the job yet. We need to interview you first. |

*(NURSEY sweeps over to the KING, feels his pulse and his head, then whips out a large thermometer, shakes it briskly and shoves it in his mouth, effectively silencing him.)*

| | |
|---|---|
| NURSEY: | He feels a bit hot. All the excitement, I expect. |
| KING BERTIE: | *(around the thermometer)* But – |
| NURSEY: | Ah ah! No talking. Nursey knows best. |

*(The KING meekly subsides.)*

| | |
|---|---|
| LORD CHAM: | My dear madam, this is the King. You really can't go round… ulp! |

*(NURSEY whips a large dummy from her apron pocket and rams it firmly in the LORD CHAMBERLAIN's mouth.)*

| | |
|---|---|
| NURSEY: | *(to the QUEEN)* There. Now we can have a nice little girly chat, eh? |
| QUEEN BETTY: | Quite so. Um – I take it you have references? |
| NURSEY: | I most certainly do. *(She fishes in her pocket and brings out a rolled scroll, which she hands to the QUEEN.)* This one's from the Duchess of Dorking. I looked after her seven children. |
| QUEEN BETTY: | Seven! Good gracious. Does she like children that much? |
| NURSEY: | No, she just loves going to PTA meetings. |
| KING BERTIE: | *(protesting)* I really don't… |
| NURSEY: | Sssh! What did I say? Under the tongue. |

*(The KING subsides.)*

| | |
|---|---|
| QUEEN BETTY: | How is your punctuality? |
| NURSEY: | Wonderful. I always get to work late, but make it up by leaving early. |
| QUEEN BETTY: | And would you say you were efficient? |
| NURSEY: | Haven't missed a coffee break for years, love. |
| QUEEN BETTY: | You'll need to work hard. |

NURSEY:            Deary, when it comes to work, I think it's fair to say
                   I'll stop at nothing.

QUEEN BETTY:       Hmm. Well, I must say, you do sound very suitable.

NURSEY:            You'll never find better. Let me tell you something.

NURSEY'S SONG
*(She sings, to the tune of 'Down In The Valley Where Nobody Goes'. As she sings, she checks the time on her watch, removes the thermometer, examines it, and replaces it in her pocket. She then produces a large bottle and spoon from her pocket and mimes dosing the horrified KING.)*

1.   If you want a nanny, and I know you do,
     Need to look no further, I'm the girl for you,
     I'm the best of the bunch, forget the rest,
     Trust in Nursey, she knows best.

2.   Wash your hands! Now! Come and eat your kippers!
     Take your shoes off! Where'd you put your slippers?
     It's a cold day! Mind you zip your zippers!
     Trust in Nursey, she knows best.

3.   I insist on manners, mind your P's and your Q's,
     There'll be no raised voices when I'm trying to snooze,
     I'm the best of the bunch, forget the rest,
     Trust in Nursey, she knows best.

4.   Is your head hot? You look a little peaky,
     Eat your soup up, lovely cock-a-leekie,
     Put your hat straight! Don't you be so cheeky!
     Trust in Nursey, she knows best.

*(At the end of the song, she swoops on the crib, swings out the sleeping baby and produces a large baby's bottle from her pocket.)*

NURSEY:            Come on, Sleeping Beauty! Bath time!

*(Exit NURSEY. KING BERTIE stares after her in horror. The LORD CHAMBERLAIN hastily removes the dummy from his mouth and hands it to the FOOTMAN. The QUEEN reads the Duchess's reference.)*

KING BERTIE:       Oh my! What a dreadful woman. What have we done?

QUEEN BETTY:       Nonsense. I thought she was charming. And this is a very
                   good reference. The Duchess says that she's an absolute
                   treasure and has a wonderful way with children.

KING BERTIE: I was hoping for someone more along the lines of Mary Poppins.

LORD CHAM: *(breaking into song)* Chim chimmenny, chim chimmeny, chim, chim, charoo. I always liked that song.

QUEEN BETTY: Well, I like Nursey. And did you hear what she called our baby? Sleeping Beauty. Isn't that a pretty name?

KING BERTIE: Hmm. What do you think, Lord Chamberlain?

LORD CHAM: Well, it beats Botty, sire.

QUEEN BETTY: Good. That's that settled. Now all we have to do is plan the Christening. I want a really good do, Bertie.

KING BERTIE: Of course, darling. Money no object.

QUEEN BETTY: A huge feast. Lots of dancing and rejoicing.

LORD CHAM: A firework display, perhaps?

KING BERTIE: Absolutely. And balloons.

QUEEN BETTY: We'll invite the twelve Good Fairies, of course. Our little Beauty might never have arrived if it wasn't for their good luck spells.

KING BERTIE: True. They can be relied upon for decent christening presents too.

QUEEN BETTY: That sounds a bit mercenary, darling.

KING BERTIE: Even so. We've got enough cuddly toys and babygros to start our own branch of Mothercare. A few Magical gifts wouldn't go amiss.

QUEEN BETTY: Mmm. What about Nightshade, though? The thirteenth Fairy. Shouldn't we invite her?

KING BERTIE: Ooer. I don't know about that. I've always found her a bit scary, to be truthful. What do you think, Lord Chamberlain?

LORD CHAM: If you want my opinion, I'd say no. A nasty piece of work, that Nightshade. Besides, there's only twelve gold plates in the best set.

QUEEN BETTY: Let's go and make out the invitations, shall we? I'll write, you stick the stamps on, Bertie. And the Lord Chamberlain can deliver them by hand.

*(QUEEN BETTY, KING BERTIE and the LORD CHAMBERLAIN exit, chattering. The FOOTMAN studies the audience.)*

FOOTMAN: It's a lousy part. But somebody has to do it.

*(Exit FOOTMAN.)*

# Act 1, Scene 2 – Invitations

*The Forest. Night time. The GOOD FAIRIES are singing and dancing.*

IN AND OUT THE DUSKY BLUEBELLS

In and out the dusky bluebells,　　Pitty pitty pat pat on your shoulder,
In and out the dusky bluebells,　　Pitty pitty pat pat on your shoulder,
In and out the dusky bluebells,　　Pitty pitty pat pat on your shoulder,
Who will be my darling?　　　　　You will be my darling.

*(Enter the LORD CHAMBERLAIN with twelve golden envelopes.)*

LORD CHAM: Charming, charming. What a delightful scene.

BLUEBELL: *(curtseying)* Good evening, Lord Chamberlain. We trust you're well?

LORD CHAM: Couldn't be better, Fairy Bluebell.

PRIMROSE: And the king and queen?

SNOWDROP: And the new baby?

LORD CHAM: All well. Now then. I have here your invitations to the Christening Party.

*(The FAIRIES squeal and clap their hands with excitement. The LORD CHAMBERLAIN distributes the invites. Each FAIRY curtsies as she receives hers.)*

LORD CHAM: Bluebell. Primrose. Snowdrop. Holly. Marigold. Poppy. Daffodil. Lilac. Rose. Iris. Willow. Violet.

*(VIOLET hesitates. The others encourage her.)*

FAIRIES:             Go on, Violet. Your turn.

*(VIOLET scurries up and collects hers.)*

FAIRIES:             *(to audience)* She's shy.

LORD CHAM:           That's it. We shall expect you all at three o'clock next
                     Saturday.

FAIRIES:             Thank you! We'll be there!

*(They skip off, singing a reprise of 'In and Out The Dusky Bluebells'. The LORD
CHAMBERLAIN watches them go with misty eyes.)*

LORD CHAM:           Charming. Utterly charming. Ah well. That's me finished
                     for the night.

*(Thunder. The lights dim. Enter NIGHTSHADE.)*

NIGHTSHADE:          Not so fast, Greybeard!

LORD CHAM:           Arrgh! You scared me.

NIGHTSHADE:          That was the general idea. Where is it, then?

LORD CHAM:           Where's what?

NIGHTSHADE:          My invitation, of course.

LORD CHAM:           Ah. Yes. Well. Er. *(He pats his pocket ineffectually.)*

NIGHTSHADE:          I haven't got one, have I?

LORD CHAM:           How can I put this? No.

NIGHTSHADE:          Typical! I seem to remember I wasn't invited to their
                     wedding either. What's the excuse this time?

LORD CHAM:           Well, I – you see, there are only twelve gold plates, and…

NIGHTSHADE:          Plates? Plates? You're blaming it on the crockery?

LORD CHAM:           Well, yes. That, and the fact that nobody likes you. Oops.

How did that slip out? I'm usually more tactful. Nerves, I suppose.

NIGHTSHADE:      Nobody likes me, eh? And why is that, pray?

LORD CHAM:      Well, without wishing to be rude, you've got a bit of a reputation for being bad, haven't you?

NIGHTSHADE:      I see. Well, old man, you haven't seen anything yet.

NIGHTSHADE'S SECOND SONG
(*NIGHTSHADE sings, to the tune of 'God Rest Ye Merry Gentlemen'*)

I'm going to make you sorrier
Than you have ever been,
So pass this message on, old man,
To both the king and queen,
I'm going to cause more trouble
Than they have ever seen,
For it just doesn't pay to cross Thirteen,
Boy, am I mean,
They'll regret having crossed Number Thirteen.

LORD CHAM:      Please, Nightshade. Don't do this. It's wicked!

NIGHTSHADE:      Go, old man! Deliver the message! Quick, before I take my temper out on you!

(*She brandishes her wand threateningly. Exit the LORD CHAMBERLAIN, in haste.*)

NIGHTSHADE:      (*to the audience*) So you think I'm nasty, eh? Well, I am! And what's more, I'm proud of it! I'm going home now, back to my cave, to hatch a wicked plan. Oh, you can boo me if you like – but I don't care. I am Nightshade, evil and deadly. Cross me at your peril!

(*She exits, cackling wildly, to the sound of thunder.*)

# Act 1, Scene 3 – The Christening

*Lights up on The Castle Throne Room. KING BERTIE and QUEEN BETTY are on their thrones. There is a large banner reading WELCOME BABY BEAUTY pinned overhead. The FOOTMAN stands to one side with a bunch of balloons, a bag of nappies and a trumpet. NURSEY stands next to the QUEEN, holding the baby, who is draped in white robes. During the song, the GUARDS, the GARDENERS, the COOK and KITCHEN STAFF parade onto the stage with flowers, trays of food and a cake.*

CELEBRATION CHRISTENING SONG
*(to the tune of 'John Brown's Body')*

1. It's time for celebration,
   Yes, the party is today,
   We have done the preparation
   And we're ready for the fray.
   Such dancing and rejoicing
   And a glorious buffet,
   It's a party, hip-hooray!

   It's a national vacation,
   Bells will ring throughout
      the nation,
   Hope you've got your invitation,
   For the party is today.

2. The guards are looking peaky,
   They've been up for half the night,
   Attending to their uniforms,
   They want to look just right,
   Their swords are sharp as razors
   And their helmets shiny bright,
   They are quite a splendid sight.

   It's a national vacation... etc

3. The gardeners have been busy,
   They have worked for days and days
   They've picked some lovely flowers
   Which they've made into bouquets,
   It isn't that surprising
   They are walking in a daze,
   They deserve a lot of praise.

   It's a national vacation...

4. The cook and all his helpers
   Have prepared a lovely spread,
   There are sausages and
      sandwiches
   And plates of gingerbread,
   They've baked a lovely cake
   That towers higher than your
      head,
   So we won't be underfed.

   It's a national vacation...

*(The song ends. The LORD CHAMBERLAIN enters.)*

LORD CHAM:          Your Majesties! The special guests have arrived!

KING BERTIE:        Excellent, excellent. Show them in, Lord Chamberlain.

*(Exit LORD CHAMBERLAIN)*

QUEEN BETTY:        I'll take the baby, Nursey.

*(NURSEY hands the baby to the QUEEN. THE FOOTMAN raises his trumpet to his lips. There is a fanfare. Enter the LORD CHAMBERLAIN.)*

LORD CHAM:          Your Majesties – The Fairies!

*(Enter THE FAIRIES. They curtsy to KING BERTIE and QUEEN BETTY.)*

BLUEBELL:           Your Majesties. We are most honoured to be invited.

QUEEN BETTY:        You're most welcome, Fairy Bluebell. It's thanks to you that our wish finally came true.

PRIMROSE:           Can we see the baby?

QUEEN BETTY:        Of course.

*(THE FAIRIES gather round, oohing and ahhing.)*

SNOWDROP:           She's so beautiful. I was going to give her the gift of beauty, but she doesn't need it.

KING BERTIE:        *(eagerly)* Gift, did you say?

QUEEN BETTY:        *(nudging him)* Sssh.

HOLLY:              We all have gifts for the baby.

MARIGOLD:           Magical ones.

KING BERTIE:        Aha! Told you.

QUEEN BETTY:        Bertie, please.

POPPY:              Would you like us to give them now?

KING BERTIE:        Absolutely. No time like the present. Ha! Did you hear what I said? I said 'There's no time like the present!'

Present. Get it? *(catches a glare from the QUEEN)* Ah.
Yes, most kind. Carry on.

DAFFODIL:               We've worked up a little routine.

LILAC:                      It's the Fairy Way.

ROSE:                       After all, it is a special occasion.

IRIS :                        Into the ring, everyone.

*(The FAIRIES kneel in a ring. VIOLET hesitates.)*

WILLOW:                  Come on, Violet. You too.

FAIRIES:                  *(to audience)* She's shy.

*(VIOLET joins the ring. As each FAIRY speaks her wish, she stands, then moves to the side.)*

BLUEBELL:               Let her be healthy and never catch 'flu.

PRIMROSE:              Let her be wealthy – and generous too.

SNOWDROP:            Let her be graceful and light on her feet.

HOLLY:                     Let her be charming to all she may meet.

MARIGOLD:             Let her have courage to stand by her word.

POPPY:                     Let her love music and sing like a bird.

DAFFODIL:               Let her be honest and never tell lies.

LILAC:                      Let her be thoughtful and let her be wise.

ROSE:                       Let her be gentle with those who are small.

IRIS :                        Let her be sunny, when rain starts to fall.

WILLOW:                  Let her be kindly and have a good heart.

*(Only VIOLET is left centre stage. She is terrified.)*

FAIRIES:                  Go on, Violet. Your turn.

*(VIOLET stands and opens her mouth to speak. There is a clap of thunder. Enter NIGHTSHADE. Lights dim. General screams and panic from everyone. The GUARDS draw their swords.)*

NIGHTSHADE:     Well, well! This is a jolly little party, isn't it? All enjoying ourselves, are we?

BLUEBELL:     What do you want, Nightshade?

NIGHTSHADE:     What do you think? I've come to see the little princess, of course! Where is she? *(spots baby)* Aha!

NURSEY:     Don't you dare touch that baby!

QUEEN BETTY:     Stay away from her! She hasn't done you any harm.

NIGHTSHADE:     Oh, but I have a gift for her! And here it is. *(She raises her wand aloft. Thunder rolls in the background)*

Upon this child, a curse I place.
Bear witness, one and all.
Across her fresh and rosy cheek
Now let the shadow fall.
For she shall live but sixteen years
And how those years will fly
Then she shall prick her finger
On a needle – and then DIE!

*(She sweeps out, leaving consternation in her wake. QUEEN BETTY bursts into tears. Everyone has forgotten that shy VIOLET has yet to speak.)*

BLUEBELL:     Wait! Quiet, everyone! Maybe Violet can help! She hasn't given her gift to the baby yet!

KING BERTIE:     Little Violet? What can she do? You heard Nightshade! Our child is doomed! Doomed!

*(Loud weeping and wailing. BLUEBELL appeals to the audience.)*

BLUEBELL:     Help us to make them quiet! After three, we'll all go sssh! Ready? One, two, three… Sssssssshhhhh!

*(The weepers and wailers subside. BLUEBELL pushes VIOLET centre stage.)*

BLUEBELL:     Go on, Violet. This is your big moment. Show them what you're made of.

| | |
|---|---|
| VIOLET: | Well, I've been thinking. I can't undo Nightshade's words, nor stop the princess from pricking her finger. But I can make the spell less dreadful. Listen. *(she raises her wand)*<br>The little princess shall not die,<br>But merely fall asleep.<br>And for one hundred years will lie<br>Inside the castle keep.<br>And when at last the years have passed,<br>She will awake once more<br>As young as when she closed her eyes,<br>And lovely as before. |
| QUEEN BETTY: | A hundred years! Oh, Bertie! Our baby! |

*(She weeps. Lights down on the sombre scene.)*

# Act 1, Scene 4 – Bad News

*Lights up on The Crossroads. Enter the TOWN CRIER.*

| | |
|---|---|
| TOWN CRIER: | Oyez! Oyez! Bad news! Bad news! Gather round! |

*(Enter THE VILLAGERS, chattering anxiously amongst themselves.)*

| | |
|---|---|
| VILLAGERS: | What did he say? Bad news? What's all this about?<br>I don't like the sound of this! |
| TOWN CRIER: | Pray silence for the King's proclamation! Know that this day, a tragedy has occurred. A curse has fallen on the head of our baby princess. |
| 1st VILLAGER: | Did he say a curse? |
| 2nd VILLAGER: | It couldn't be worse! |
| VILLAGERS: | Ssssh! |
| TOWN CRIER: | Princess Beauty has been threatened by the evil Fairy Nightshade. If she pricks her finger between now and her sixteenth birthday, she will fall asleep for one hundred years. |
| VILLAGERS: | What? Oh no! Poor little thing! How cruel! |
| TOWN CRIER: | In the hopes that this tragedy can be avoided, the King |

has made a new law. From this day forward, all needles and pins are banned throughout the kingdom.

VILLAGERS:  No needles or pins?
Oh dear! Oh no!
But how will we spin?
And how will we sew?
What'll we do
To mend our clothes
When we're all in rags
And the cold wind blows?
If needles and pins
Are both taboo,
What'll we do?
Oh, what'll we do?

*(Thunder, flashing lights. Enter NIGHTSHADE, to general consternation.)*

NIGHTSHADE:  You'll freeze, that's what! You'll spend the next sixteen winters shivering around your pathetic fires in worn out rags! And you know what? I'll be laughing at you! Because it won't make the slightest difference! A curse is a curse, and it'll take more than a stupid royal decree to lift it!

NIGHTSHADE'S THIRD SONG
*(To the tune of 'God Rest Ye Merry Gentlemen')*

When Nightshade is insulted
Then all must pay the price,
It doesn't do to cross me,
My heart is cold as ice,
I bear a grudge for ever,
So here is my advice
Go on home, lock your doors, for I'm not nice,
Not at all nice,
You've dishonoured me
And all must pay the price! Ha, ha, ha, ha, ha!

*(The TOWN CRIER and VILLAGERS exit, screaming. Lights down on the triumphant NIGHTSHADE.)*

**INTERVAL**

# Act 2, Scene 1 – Birthday Celebrations

*The Castle Kitchen. It is sixteen years later – on BEAUTY's birthday. The COOK is rolling out pastry on a table. The KITCHEN STAFF are arranging food on platters. The GUARDS stand to attention by the birthday cake, which stands on another cloth-covered table. Unbeknown to the audience, Beauty is hiding beneath. The GARDENERS are bustling about with baskets of flowers.*

CELEBRATION BIRTHDAY SONG
*(All sing, to the tune of 'John Brown's Body')*

> Today is Beauty's birthday,
> She is sweet sixteen at last,
> And everyone's forgotten
> All the troubles of the past,
> So let the bells ring out
> And hoist the flag on up the mast,
> For she's sweet sixteen at last.
>
> It's a national vacation,
> Bells will ring across the nation,
> Join with us in celebration,
> For she's sweet sixteen at last!

*Enter KING BERTIE, QUEEN BETTY, the LORD CHAMBERLAIN and the FOOTMAN, who is staggering under the weight of a large, bulging treasure chest. Strings of pearls hang over the sides.)*

| | |
|---|---|
| LORD CHAM: | … and as you can see, Your Majesties, everything's on schedule in the kitchen. The staff have been up all night preparing, isn't that right, cook? |
| COOK: | *(yawning)* Quite right, sir. |
| KING BERTIE: | Hmm. Be wanting overtime, will they? |
| COOK: | Oh, no, sire. Nothing's too much trouble for our little Princess Beauty, sire. She's everybody's favourite. |
| KING BERTIE: | That's the spirit. Er – what are the guards doing here? |
| COOK: | Guarding the cake, sire. I don't trust nobody, I don't. |

LORD CHAM:     Ah. Guardians of the gate-o, eh? Get it? Gate-o. Gateau. (*Blank faces all round*) Oh never mind.

QUEEN BETTY:     Oh, Bertie. Can you believe it? Our little Beauty, sixteen years old today. Let's go and look in the treasure chest. I want to choose something really pretty for her. After all, this is her coming-out party.

LORD CHAM:     My sister had a coming-out party, but they made her go in again...

(*QUEEN BETTY marches out, tugging KING BERTIE behind her. The FOOTMAN trails behind, as always, clutching the chest. He accidentally kicks a bread roll which has fallen to the floor. The LORD CHAMBERLAIN steps on it unwittingly.*)

LORD CHAM:     I'll just stay here and tell a few more amusing jokes. I feel I'm on a roll. (*Picks up the bread roll and flourishes it merrily.*)

(*Offstage, NURSEY's voice can be heard bellowing.*)

NURSEY:     Beauty! Beauty, where are you?

LORD CHAM:     On second thoughts...

(*He hastily exits. Enter NURSEY.*)

NURSEY:     Has anyone seen Beauty? Ooh! Birthday cake! My favourite!

(*She reaches out to the cake. The GUARDS whip out their swords.*)

NURSEY:     On the other hand, perhaps I'll stick with spinach. Less fattening and it puts colour in your cheeks.

BEAUTY:     Do you want green cheeks, then, Nursey?

(*Laughing, she comes out from under the table.*)

NURSEY:     Ooh, you naughty! I've been looking for you everywhere!

BEAUTY:     Well, that's the whole point of hide-and-seek, isn't it?

NURSEY: But I told you not to come into the kitchen! There's secrets going on.

BEAUTY: Well, where can I go? I'm not allowed into the throne room, because they're putting up the balloons and I can't go in the hall because they're rolling out the red carpet for the guests.

NURSEY: What's wrong with the garden?

BEAUTY: Mother says I mustn't get my new dress dirty.

NURSEY: Well, that's just the way of it. We're doing all this for you, you know.

BEAUTY: I know. I'm grateful, really I am. But it's so boring, waiting for the party to begin. I'll burst with excitement if I don't do something. Can I stay and help, Cook? Please?

COOK: Oh no, Miss Beauty. More than my job's worth.

BEAUTY: I can help guard the cake from Nursey.

NURSEY: Don't you be so cheeky. Now, run along. I want a word with Cook.

BEAUTY: Oh, come on, Nursey. Please play hide-and-seek. Please, please, please. Pretty please with knobs on.

NURSEY: You start, I'll be along in a minute. Now, Cook, remember. Don't taste the food while you're cooking it, or you'll lose the nerve to serve it.

COOK: Madam, I'll have you know I've been cooking for ten years!

NURSEY: Then you ought to be done by now. *(Pokes her finger in a trifle.)* By the way, what's this on the plate? In case I have to describe it to the doctor?

COOK: I have never been so insulted in my life.

*(He chases NURSEY off stage, brandishing the rolling pin. Their shrieks die away. The KITCHEN STAFF and GARDENERS carry on with their work.*

*BEAUTY snaps her fingers under the noses of the GUARDS. They don't move a muscle. She sighs and moves to front of stage. Lights down on the Kitchen. She is lit by a spot.)*

TODAY IS MY BIRTHDAY
*(BEAUTY sings, to the tune of 'On Top Of Old Smokey')*

1.  Today is my birthday,
    I've got a new dress,
    I guess you could call me
    A lucky princess.
    I'm having a party,
    It's starting at three,
    But everyone's busy
    With no time for me.

2.  I'm feeling quite dizzy
    All fizzy inside,
    They tell me, calm down, girl
    And be dignified.
    But I'm so excited
    And carried away,
    Today is my birthday,
    I'm sixteen today.

# Act 2, Scene 2 – The Curse

*(Thunder. Lights up on the Tower Room. NIGHTSHADE, wearing a long black hooded cloak sits hunched over a spinning wheel. There is a pile of yellow flax at her feet. There is a small couch. BEAUTY stands at the foot of the steps leading up to the stage.)*

BEAUTY: It's all very well for them. They've got things to do. But what about me? I can't just wander around twiddling my fingers until three o'clock... oh! What's that curious little door? I've never noticed that before!

*(She moves towards the Tower Room. Thunder rumbles ominously.)*

NIGHTSHADE: That's right. Come on, my little Beauty. Come to Nightshade... closer... closer...

BEAUTY: This looks like the perfect place for hide-and-seek. Nursey will never find me here... oh!

*(She enters the Tower Room and spots NIGHTSHADE.)*

BEAUTY: Who are you?

NIGHTSHADE: Oh, nobody important. Just a harmless old woman, spinning away. Spin, spin, spinning away.

| | |
|---|---|
| BEAUTY: | Spinning? Is that what you call it? |
| NIGHTSHADE: | Why, yes. Haven't you ever seen a spinning wheel before, deary? |
| BEAUTY: | Well, no. Is it difficult to work? |
| NIGHTSHADE: | It's very easy, my pretty little lady. When you know how. |
| BEAUTY: | Could I try, please? |
| NIGHTSHADE: | Of course. Come closer. Sit. *(BEAUTY sits.)* Put your foot on the pedal – so – and hold the thread – so – and the wheel will spin round. |

*(BEAUTY does as instructed. She reaches out her hand and pricks her finger on the spindle. She jumps up.)*

| | |
|---|---|
| BEAUTY: | Oh! I've pricked my finger! |
| NIGHTSHADE: | Just as I said you would! Ha, ha, ha, ha, ha! |

*(With a triumphant cackle, she throws back her cloak to reveal herself. She seizes her wand and brandishes it on high. She speaks directly to the audience)*

My wicked curse has come to pass!
I've waited sixteen years!
Remember when I told you
That this tale would end in tears?
Go home, my friends! Go home and weep.
The play now ends. What's left is sleep.
Ha, ha, ha, ha!

*(NIGHTSHADE exits, to thunder. BEAUTY, clutching her finger, moves, swaying, towards the couch.)*

| | |
|---|---|
| BEAUTY: | What's happening to me? I feel – so – terribly – sleepy... |

*(She collapses on the couch. Lights down.)*

# Act 2, Scene 3 – Time Passes

*Lights up on the Kitchen. There is a frozen tableau. KING BERTIE, QUEEN BETTY, the LORD CHAMBERLAIN and the FOOTMAN have returned. the QUEEN holds the necklace she has selected for BEAUTY. The COOK and*

*NURSEY are also present, frozen in the act of running. The COOK's rolling pin is suspended over NURSEY's head. The GUARDS, KITCHEN STAFF and GARDENERS are asleep where they stand.*

*Enter the SPIDERS. They perform a dance in which they drape cobwebs over the sleepers. At the end of the dance, everyone is covered in cobwebs. The SPIDERS exit. The music fades away, to be replaced by the sound of a slowly ticking clock. Enter FAIRY VIOLET. She addresses the audience directly.*

VIOLET:     Oh dear. It rather seems I'm in the limelight again.
         All the others say I've got to do it, because it's my spell.
         So here goes. Ahem.

         A silent castle. Nothing stirs.
         The spiders spin and creep.
         Outside the walls, the world moves on.
         Yet still the sleepers sleep.
         The years go by and still they dream
         The trees grow wild and free
         In time, the mighty castle
         Starts to fade from memory.
         Will Beauty never wake? you cry
         Will evil Nightshade win?
         Just watch. A hundred years roll by –
         And now, my spell kicks in.

*(Exit VIOLET. Lights down.)*

# Act 2, Scene 4 – The Prince

*Lights up on The Forest. A great deal of tangled thicket has sprung up over the years. The TOWN CRIER, now a 130 year-old ancient, sporting spectacles and a long grey beard, snores at the foot of a tree.*

VALENTINE:    *(off stage)* Hi there! Anybody need any help? Anybody lost in the forest? Can I be of assistance to anyone?

*(PRINCE VALENTINE bounds on stage and strikes a pose. He addresses the audience directly).*

VALENTINE:    Ta da! Here I am. One handsome prince, all ready for action. Hair in place, trusty sword drawn and generally looking gooood.

*(He inspects himself in the mirrored back of the shield. The TOWN CRIER comes awake rubbing his eyes blearily.)*

TOWN CRIER:     Oy oy! What's all the racket about? Can't an old fellow snatch forty winks?

VALENTINE:      Hi there, old timer. Prince Valentine at your service. Any dragons need slaying? Maidens rescuing? Quests need questing? All in a day's work for yours truly.

TOWN CRIER:     Clear off, you noisy young varmint with your daft tights.

VALENTINE:      Hey, hey, hey! That's no way to talk to royalty.

TOWN CRIER:     I'm a hundred and thirty years old. I'll talk how I like.

VALENTINE:      Wow! A hundred and thirty, eh? I wouldn't have put you a day over ninety.

TOWN CRIER:     I was in me prime at ninety. Still working.

VALENTINE:      And what did you do, old greybeard?

TOWN CRIER:     I was the Town Crier hereabouts. Took on the job when I was fourteen. Fine pair o' lungs I had. 'Course, the voice has gone now. The old memory's not what it once was either. There's three things I can't remember. Names, faces – and I've forgotten the third. *(Valentine is craning his neck to look through the thicket)* Are you listening to me, young feller?

VALENTINE:      Yes. I just thought I caught a glimpse of a tower in the distance. Look, there. See?

TOWN CRIER:     I'm a hundred and thirty, son. I can't see past the end of me nose.

VALENTINE:      Have your eyes ever been checked?

TOWN CRIER:     Nope, they've always been brown. Do stop craning your neck like that. It's very irritating.

VALENTINE:      You know, it's a great shame about your bad memory. I was hoping to pick your brains, you being so old and everything. I hoped you might know something about the princess.

TOWN CRIER: Princess?

VALENTINE: I overheard them talking at the inn. Some old story about an enchanted princess, who lies under a spell in some castle hereabouts. It sounds like my kind of thing. I don't suppose this would help jog your memory?

*(VALENTINE takes a bag of gold from his pocket and jingles it suggestively. The TOWN CRIER snatches it eagerly.)*

TOWN CRIER: Funnily enough, it's all coming back to me now. Yes, young sir. There was a princess. Beauty was her name. And a lovely young lass she were. Shame she went to sleep. It was the curse, see. Was I asleep just now, by the way?

VALENTINE: Yes, yes, I woke you up. Carry on about the princess.

TOWN CRIER: What princess?

VALENTINE: You were telling me about a princess under a curse.

TOWN CRIER: Was I? I dunno. My memory.

*(VALENTINE produces another bag of gold.)*

VALENTINE: Might this do the trick?

TOWN CRIER: *(snatching it)* Very kind, young sir, very kind. What was it you wanted to know?

VALENTINE: About the curse.

TOWN CRIER: Aye. The curse. It was laid on her by a wicked fairy, see. We weren't allowed to use needles. It was important that she didn't prick her finger, because if she did, she'd fall asleep for a hundred years. They were very worried about it, up at the castle. Matter of fact, it was me who read out the decree.

VALENTINE: Where was the castle?

| | |
|---|---|
| TOWN CRIER: | *(pointing)* It lay that a-way. |
| VALENTINE: | I knew it! That is a tower I can see! |
| TOWN CRIER: | Aye. There was a road leading to it back in the old days. Long grown over now. Place'll be in ruins, I should think. What you doing now? |

*(VALENTINE approaches the thicket, takes a comb from his pocket and arranges his hair, using the back of his shield as a mirror.)*

| | |
|---|---|
| VALENTINE: | I'm going to take a look. This sounds like a job for Valentine. |
| TOWN CRIER: | You'll ladder your tights, tryin' to get through that lot. |

*(PRINCE VALENTINE begins hacking determinedly at the undergrowth.)*

| | |
|---|---|
| VALENTINE: | I'll take my chances! Thanks for the information, old timer. Wish me luck. |

*(VALENTINE vanishes into the thicket.)*

| | |
|---|---|
| TOWN CRIER: | *(to the audience)* I'd best be off home in case he changes his mind. *(He exits.)* |

# Act 2, Scene 5 – The Happy Ending

*Lights up on the Castle Kitchen. Everyone is in the same position, covered with cobwebs. Enter VALENTINE, sword in hand.*

| | |
|---|---|
| VALENTINE: | Wow! Weirdsville! |

*(He walks up to KING BERTIE and gingerly lifts the cobweb. He snaps his fingers under BERTIE's nose.)*

| | |
|---|---|
| VALENTINE: | Hey! Wake up! |

*(There is no response. VALENTINE lifts the cobweb from QUEEN BETTY. He gives her a little shake.)*

| | |
|---|---|
| VALENTINE: | Your Majesty! Rise and shine! |

*(Again, there is no response. VALENTINE addresses the audience.)*

VALENTINE:        What's happened here?

*(Shaking his head in bewilderment, he walks around removing the cobwebs from the LORD CHAMBERLAIN, the FOOTMAN and finally, NURSEY.)*

VALENTINE:        Good grief! This is like some kind of horror story.

*(Lights up on the Tower Room, where BEAUTY lies sleeping. VALENTINE notices the door.)*

VALENTINE:        I wonder where that goes?

*(Slowly, he walks up the steps and enters the Tower Room. Immediately, he spots the sleeping princess.)*

VALENTINE:        Wow! So this is her. The old man was right. She's gorgeous. *(He combs his hair again, takes a bottle of breath freshener from his pocket and sprays his mouth. Gently, he shakes her shoulder.)* Your Highness! Princess Beauty! Wake up!

*(BEAUTY doesn't stir. In despair, VALENTINE sinks to one knee. He picks up one limp, dangling hand. He turns and addresses the audience.)*

VALENTINE:        Shall I?

AUDIENCE:        Yes!

VALENTINE:        You think it might work?

AUDIENCE:        Yes!

VALENTINE:        Okay then. Here goes.

*(He kisses her hand. There is a long pause. Then, slowly, BEAUTY sits up and stretches.)*

BEAUTY:        Goodness. I must have dozed off for a moment. What a strange dream. *(She notices VALENTINE.)* Oh! Who are you?

VALENTINE:        Prince Valentine at your service, Your Highness.

Daredevil, tough guy and all-round hero. Can I call you Beauty?

BEAUTY: But how did you get in?

VALENTINE: Oh, just fought my way through a mighty thicket of thorns. Nothing to it. Not even any dragons or ogres guarding the portal.

BEAUTY: You do this sort of thing often?

VALENTINE: Oh, yes. I've rescued a few maidens in my time. But I've never felt like settling down, you know? Until now.

BEAUTY: *(to audience)* Wow. He's cool!

*(Lights down in the Tower Room. Simultaneously, everyone in the Kitchen wakes, yawning and stretching. Everyone deposits their cobwebs with the FOOTMAN, then carries on with what they were doing as though never interrupted.)*

COOK: Criticise my cooking, would you?

*(He brings the rolling pin down on NURSEY's head.)*

NURSEY: Ouch! Get away, you big bully! Did you see that, everybody? I've got a great big lump on me noddle!

LORD CHAM: Well, I suggest you keep it under your hat. Excuse me. I think I hear the doorbell.

*(Exit LORD CHAMBERLAIN.)*

QUEEN BETTY: I definitely think this green necklace is the prettiest, don't you, darling?

KING BERTIE: If you say so, darling. I would have preferred cricket stumps at her age, but there's no accounting for taste.

QUEEN BETTY: Oh my! Here she comes. Quick, hide it away!

*(KING BERTIE panics. NURSEY snatches the necklace and hides it in her pocket as BEAUTY and PRINCE VALENTINE enter.)*

QUEEN BETTY: Hallo, darling. Where have you been?

KING BERTIE:      What's more to the point, who's that?

BEAUTY:      I had a little nap up in the Tower Room. And this is Valentine, my fiancé.

ALL:      Fiancé?

NURSEY:      Ooh, my little poppet! I hear wedding bells!

*(She rushes to BEAUTY and hugs both her and PRINCE VALENTINE.)*

KING BERTIE:      Tower Room? I thought that was where we kept the old sofas and stuff. Did you know there was a fiancé up there, Betty?

QUEEN BETTY:      Well, no. I must say this is all very unexpected, darling. Have you known each other long?

BEAUTY:      No. I just woke up, and there he was. Calm down, Daddy. He's a prince with his own castle and everything.

KING BERTIE:      What's he doing in ours, then?

VALENTINE:      Well sire, I've been roaming the world for the last couple of years. Righting wrongs, slaying monsters, rescuing damsels in distress, that sort of thing.

KING BERTIE:      How many damsels?

VALENTINE:      Loads. But none of them hold a candle to your daughter. I'd be deeply honoured if I could have her hand in marriage, sire. *(He bows deeply)*

NURSEY:      Oooh! Lovely manners!

KING BERTIE:      Well, I don't know what to think. There's something very odd about all this…

*(Enter the LORD CHAMBERLAIN.)*

LORD CHAM:      Excuse me, your Majesties. We have visitors.

QUEEN BETTY:      It's three o'clock already? Where did the time go?

*(Enter THE TWELVE GOOD FAIRIES.)*

| | |
|---|---|
| KING BERTIE: | Wonderful to see you! I'm awfully sorry, you've rather caught us on the hop. Something odd seems to have happened to the time today… |
| BLUEBELL: | It's all right, your Majesty. You don't have to explain. In fact, there's something we should explain to you. |
| SNOWDROP: | Don't be shy, Violet. Do it in poetry. You're good at that. |

*(VIOLET stands stage centre. Everyone listens in amazement as she speaks.)*

| | |
|---|---|
| VIOLET: | You've been asleep one hundred years.<br>That's why you're all at sea.<br>If you will just be patient,<br>I will jog your memory.<br>The evil Nightshade's wicked curse<br>Was softened with my spell.<br>And on behalf of all of us<br>I'm glad things turned out well.<br>For Good has triumphed here today<br>And right has conquered wrong.<br>This is the ending of our play.<br>Except for one last song! |

**FINAL SONG**
*(to the tune of John Brown's Body)*

1.  We hope you have enjoyed yourselves,
    And had some fun tonight,
    We might have missed a line or two,
    But mostly got it right.
    You've been a lovely audience,
    Attentive and polite,
    In fact, a real delight.
    Thank you, everyone, for coming,
    Hope we send you homeward humming,
    Thank you everyone, for coming,
    You've been a real delight.

*(The cast take their bows as the piano plays. When everyone is on stage, there is a final reprise of the song.)*

**THE END**

# Staging

## Area for Performance

If you have a fixed stage, you can of course create extra areas by using rostra blocks to build out on either side, as shown in the picture below. If you have a hall with a fixed stage and no means of extending this, you will need to keep your set design as simple as possible, to avoid long waits between scenes.

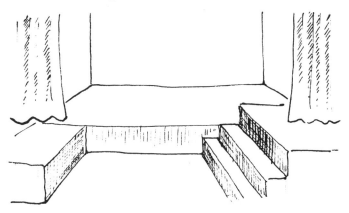

The advantage of the arrangement shown in the picture is that the central area only requires one scene change, which occurs during the interval. In Act 1, it is the Castle Throne Room. In Act 2, it becomes the Castle Kitchen. The area on the left remains The Forest throughout the play, with the addition of some extra undergrowth in Act 2, Scene 4. (See under Scenery and Props – The Forest.) The area on the right doubles up as The Crossroads and The Tower Room. Ideally, the area on the right should be higher than the other two areas, with steps leading up to it. The steps are useful in the Crossroads scenes, to provide more space for the Villagers to congregate. Also, Beauty and Prince Valentine can be seen ascending them in scenes featuring the Tower Room.

## Backdrops

It is certainly not necessary to have backdrops. A simple way to indicate a location is to have an actor – the Footman, perhaps – parade across the acting area carrying a sign, eg THE CASTLE THRONE ROOM. However, backdrops can be very effective and can be simply made by sticking together large sheets of paper with masking tape. The Forest area could show a path winding through the trees with the towers of the castle in the distance. The Throne Room becomes The Kitchen in Act 2. If you do not wish to change backdrops, a large painting of draped curtains showing a view of the grounds from a window would suffice for both. The third area doubles as the Village Crossroads and the Tower Room. If you wish to create a different backdrop for each scene, the first could show the timbered houses of the village in the distance and the second could depict the shadowy interior of the Tower Room.

# Scenery and Props

A great many characters appear on stage at any one time, therefore it is best to keep props and scenery to a minimum. Here are some ideas:

## The Forest

If you have space, you may like to include one or two free-standing cut out trees. Cut the tree shapes from strong cardboard, paint or decorate them and support them at the back with a strong cardboard support in the following way.

Alternatively, you can use artificial Christmas trees – or even children, if you are looking to expand the numbers of parts.

In the final Forest scene, one hundred years worth of tangled undergrowth has appeared, through which Prince Valentine has to fight his way. A simple way of doing this would be to bring on two lightweight screens, painted and/or covered with creepers and ivy. He can slip between the two and vanish. If you are using children as trees, they can be bunched together and Valentine can force his way between them.

## The Crossroads

A free-standing sign can be made from wood or strong cardboard, with three arms pointing to The Castle, The Village and The Forest.

## The Throne Room

Two thrones are required for this set. Two chairs with arms can have high, gold painted cardboard backs attached with string. The lower parts of the chairs can be concealed with gold paper.

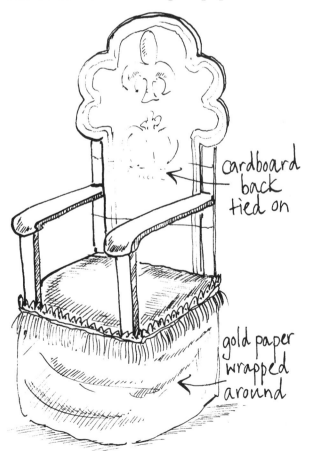

# Scenery and Props

Scene 1 also requires a lavishly decorated crib for the baby, which is a doll wrapped in a lacy shawl. To make the crib, stick three cardboard boxes together, one inside the other, the third makes a base. Cover the boxes with pink fabric or crepe paper. Fix a tall pole to one end and hang more fabric or crepe paper from the top. Decorate with ribbons.

During Scene 3, a banner is displayed with the words WELCOME BABY BEAUTY. This can be pinned to the backdrop. Also, a tall Christening cake is paraded on stage. This can be made from circular boxes stuck on top of the other, gradually decreasing in size. They can be painted white and decorated with pink edging. The Cook can carry it in on a firm base, to which it can be stuck to avoid accidents. Platters of food are also brought onstage by the Kitchen Staff. This can be made from papier mâché and decorated accordingly. The same food can double up for the birthday party in Act 2.

**The Castle Kitchen**

This set requires a table, at which the cook is rolling out pastry. Another table or surface is also necessary, displaying platters of food being prepared by the kitchen staff. The Christening cake from Scene 3 can double as a birthday cake by placing a cardboard ring on top mounted with sixteen candles. The table on which it stands needs to be covered with a cloth, as Beauty is hiding beneath.

During this scene, the Footman carries on a large treasure chest, dripping with jewels. This can be made from a cardboard box, painted brown and embellished with cut out pieces of gold foil.

**The Tower Room**

This set requires a small couch, a chair or stool for Nightshade, a pile of flax (yellow raffia) and a spinning wheel.

## Props

It is a good idea to set up a table backstage, from which the actors collect the props they need for each scene. The small props required are as follows:

**Prologue**

Twelve wands for the Fairies.
Wand for Nightshade.

# Scenery and Props

Bell for the Town Crier.
Pitchforks, crooks, baskets for Villagers.
**Act 1, scene 1**
Doll, wrapped in a shawl.
An armful of cuddly toys, rattles, etc,
for Footman. Must include a duck
and a pink rabbit.
A long feather for the King.
A huge thermometer, a large dummy,
a scroll, a bottle of medicine and spoon,
and a large baby's bottle for Nursey's
apron pocket.
**Act 1, scene 2**
12 golden envelopes for the Lord
Chamberlain.
**Act 1, scene 3**
Doll in Christening robe for Nursey.
A bunch of balloons, a bag of nappies
and a trumpet for Footman.
Artificial flowers for Gardeners.
Swords for Guards.
Trays of food for the Kitchen Staff.
A tall cake.
**Act 1, scene 4**
Bell for Town Crier.
Pitchforks/crooks/baskets for Villagers.
**Act 2, scene 1**
Rolling pin/pastry for Cook.
Platters of food for Kitchen Staff.
Tall cake with 16 candles.
Artificial flowers for Gardeners.
Treasure chest for Footman.
Green necklace.
A bread roll.
**Act 2, scene 2**
A pile of yellow flax (raffia).
Spinning wheel.
**Act 2, scene 3**
Rolling pin for cook.
Cobwebs for Spiders *(see Costume)*.

**Act 2, scene 4**
Spectacles for Town Crier *(see Costume)*.
Sword, heart shaped shield, comb, mouth
spray and two bags of gold for Prince.

Some of these props are easy to find,
but a few will need to be made.

**Rolling Pin**
The Cook actually whacks Nursey on
the head with this, so it needs to be
constructed of papier mâché layered onto
a cardboard tube from a kitchen roll.

**Swords**
You can construct these from stiff
cardboard covered with silver foil.

**Pitchforks/crooks**
Bind foil-covered cardboard prongs
or crooks on to long poles.

**Nursey's Thermometer**
This needs to be comically large. Use a
bulb baster, replacing the bulb with a
smaller, foil-covered sphere.

**Valentine's Shield**
Cut a large heart shape from thick
cardboard. Paint one side pink and
decorate with cut out hearts. Cover the
back with silver foil. Staple a strip of
thick elastic to the back, as a hand grip.

# Lighting

If your school has a stage, you may well have theatrical lighting with floods and spots. It is possible to hire equipment, if you have an adult prepared to supervise this. However, it is not essential to use theatrical lighting. Ceiling lights can be switched off during scene changes and there are moments during the play when it would be effective to switch them off and on again, such as at the entrance of Nightshade.

# Casting and Auditions

## Casting the Parts

This calls for a good deal of diplomacy. Not everyone can have a starring role – but then again, when you explain the commitment needed to learn a great number of lines and regularly attend rehearsals, not everyone will want one. However, anyone who is keen should be allowed to try for a part. The fair way is to hold auditions.

I suggest you hold an initial meeting with everyone who wishes to be involved, in whatever capacity. Remind them of the story of Sleeping Beauty and tell them about the Main Characters *(see pages 42 and 43.)* Some of the roles are quite challenging and will involve a great deal of hard work and staying power. Those who take on smaller roles will also be spending a lot of time in rehearsal.

Point out that there are interesting alternatives to acting. Some children may be talented musicians or singers and will prefer to be a member of the choir or orchestra. You will also need an efficient Stage Management team. Scenery needs to be designed and painted. Props must be made. Make it clear that every aspect of a production is vitally important.

# *Casting and Auditions*

## The Auditions

Here are some drama exercises to help you explore the natural acting talents of your cast. At this stage, you are looking for concentration and the ability to become immersed in a role.

• Describe the sort of activities that may be taking place in the palace just before Beauty pricks her finger. The Guards are marching, the Gardeners are picking flowers, the Kitchen Staff are preparing food, the King and Queen are selecting a birthday gift for Beauty. Ask them to choose their character and keep it a secret. You want to guess who they are and what they are doing from their actions. At a given signal, they become their character and improvise the appropriate activity. They do this collectively. At a second signal – representing the moment in time when Beauty's finger is pricked – they fall asleep.

• Divide the children into small groups. Tell them that they are attending a Town Crier's convention. Provide a bell, which will be passed around. Within each group, when the bell is in their hand, they must stand and deliver a short piece of news in their best Town Crier manner. Each child will decide for him or herself what news they wish to divulge. It is the bold, self-confident delivery that counts.

• Divide the children into groups of three. Provide a doll. Ask them to improvise a scene where The King,

The Queen and Nursey are arguing about a suitable name for the baby. The suggestions should include some very silly names and the "baby" should be very much a part of the scene. Give the groups plenty of time to work out their improvisation and explore their characters before they perform it to you. Natural comedians will be spotted instantly.

• Now make them work in pairs. Ask them to improvise the scene in the forest where the Lord Chamberlain is accosted by Nightshade, the thirteenth fairy. She demands her invitation to the Christening and the Lord Chamberlain is forced to admit that she doesn't have one. The Lord Chamberlain should show his fear, and Nightshade her rage.

You should now have some idea which children have a natural presence and will be able to handle the more challenging roles. At this point, hand out the scripts and arrange to have a "read-through" the following day. Allow the children to try reading different parts before making your final decision. Announce forthcoming auditions for singers, dancers and members of the orchestra, so that any keen performers who haven't secured an acting part can attend those. Arrange to have a meeting with all those who may be interested in back stage work.

# The Main Characters

**The Twelve Good Fairies**
Sweet-natured, concerned and helpful. They find Nightshade's attitude quite shocking.

**Nightshade – the thirteenth Fairy**
Malicious, mocking and resentful. She takes great pleasure in her wickedness.

**King Bertie**
A very keen first-time dad, but rather ineffectual. He generally leaves all the important decisions to his wife.

**Princess Beauty**
Charming, high-spirited and good-natured, with a sense of fun.

**Queen Betty**
The Queen wears the trousers in this household. She knows her own mind and can be a little brisk at times.

**Nursey**
The traditional pantomime dame role. Larger than life. Ideally should be played by a boy.

### The Kitchen Staff
The Cook's helpers. Always busily arranging food on platters, sweeping up or whisking things in bowls.

### The Cook
Very proud of his culinary abilities. Doesn't take kindly to criticism.

### The Lord Chamberlain
An organiser. Very loyal. Has a dry wit.

### The Footman
Doomed to hold and carry things with very little reward.

### The Spiders
Slow moving, rather sinister.

### The Town Crier
In Act 1, he is a smart youth possessed of a huge voice. In Act 2, he has aged one hundred years and has become a feeble old man with an unreliable memory which can only be jogged by gold.

### The Gardeners
A hard-working team who are never seen without armfuls of flowers and greenery.

### The Guards
Business-like, well-trained and efficient.

### Prince Valentine
A dashing hero. Very over the top. Can be played by either sex.

# The Stage Management Team

An ideal stage management team should consist of at least eight children with specific tasks. They should be involved in rehearsals at an early stage.

**Director's Assistant**
Your right-hand man or woman. Their job will be to make lists, post rehearsal schedules, chase things up, take messages and remind you of things.

**Scene Shifters**
Two or more children are needed to carry large props and pieces of scenery on and off stage and change backdrops or close curtains as necessary.

**Props Table**
One team member should take responsibility for the backstage props table, making sure that all items are assembled on the table, ready for the actors to collect prior to their entrance.

**Lighting**
If theatrical lighting is used, an adult will supervise this. An assistant may be useful. If you are using ceiling lights, one team member can be respond during scene changes and at appro-priate points during the play. He or she will require a script marked with the lighting cues.

**Prompter**
This job calls for an alert individual, who can be positioned inconspicuously with a copy of the script, ready to supply the line if necessary. The prompter will doubtless end up by knowing the play backwards – a useful emergency understudy!

**Sound Effects**
There are several occasions in the play where live sound effects are called for (see page 48). There are also places where recorded music/sound effects are needed. One or two members of the team should take responsibility for producing the live effects and managing the tape recorder.

**Front Of House**
Two team members can be made responsible for arranging the seating, greeting the audience as they arrive, distributing programmes and possibly passing around a collecting tin at the end.

## Rehearsal Schedule

Decide well in advance the date for your performance. Draw up a schedule of rehearsals, including a technical run through (when the stage management team are put through their paces) and a dress rehearsal. The children will need plenty of forewarning if they are required to attend at lunchtime or after school. In the early stages, do not try to get every scene perfect before moving on to the next one. Keep pushing on, otherwise you may find that the later scenes are under-rehearsed and the earlier ones have gone stale.

# Costume

Here are some simple suggestions.

## Female roles

### The Twelve Good Fairies

Each Fairy has a specific flower name, so the colour of her costume is self-evident. Green tights or leggings would be effective. Each can wear a simple, short tunic cut from crepe paper in the appropriate shade, with matching paper flowers attached to a headband. Tie a few small bells to each wand (a silver star stuck on the end of a stick) so that they make a magical sound when waved. Wings are an optional extra.

### Nightshade

Make Nightshade's outfit by attaching long strips of black and purple material to a collar. She can wear the traditional pointed witch hat if you like – or a wild purple-and-black fright wig made out of wool fastened onto a headband. She needs a hooded cloak for the scene in the Tower room. Her wand has a black star. Black or purple lipstick and eyeliner will make her a force to be reckoned with.

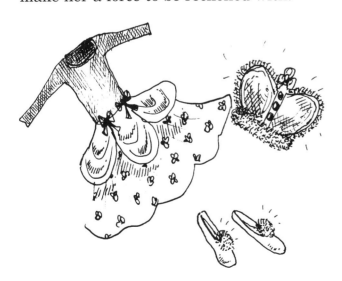

### Queen Betty

An old bridesmaid's dress or cut-down evening dress would be ideal. Add plenty of jewellery and a crown made as follows:

Use a strip of card about 6cm wide to make the headband. Cut two strips of gold card about 3cm thick and 50cm long to make the top of the crown. Bend the strips across each other and tape the ends to the inside of the headband. Push a piece of colourful crepe paper into the crown and tape it in place. Glue a strip of cotton wool around the headband and dot with black felt pen.

scrunchy crepe paper

### Beauty

A bridesmaid's dress would be ideal, but an effective dress can be made from a leotard and two skirts. One is the underskirt. The overskirt can be bunched up and pinned to the underskirt with large safety pins covered with bows. The leotard top can be suitably decorated. She can wear ballet slippers with attached tinsel pom-poms on her feet. A sparkly coronet will complete her outfit.

# Costume

## Male roles

### King Bertie
The King needs a royal cloak with a white, ruffled shirt beneath and rolled-up leggings over tights on his lower half. Trim his shoes with ribbons. Give him a crown similar to the Queen's.

### The Lord Chamberlain
A plain, black, floorlength robe would be perfect. He is referred to as Greybeard, so he should either have a false beard or be made up appropriately.

### The Town Crier
A black or red jacket, trimmed with braid, teamed with matching leggings rolled up to the knee and worn over a pair of tights should do the trick. Make him a tricorn hat from black card and attach large ribbons to his shoes. He needs a good-sized hand bell. Maybe the school bell? When he ages 116 years, he will need spectacle frames and a long beard, which can be constructed from grey wool and hooked around his ears with elastic.

### The Cook
Should be dressed in a white apron with a cook's hat. This can be made in the same way as the King's and Queen's crowns, using a white card headband and two crossbands with white crepe paper pushed inside.

## Unisex roles

### The Footman
He requires breeches (those old rolled up leggings again!) and a matching jacket, or white, flouncy blouse with ruffles and a waistcoat over the top. A wig can be made from white raffia attached to a headband and gathered up behind in a short pony tail with a large black ribbon.

glue on lengths of raffia

wide, solid hairband

gather into bow, trim neatly

### Nursey
Although this character is a female, traditionally it is played by a male. The costume consists of a basic blue dress (heavily stuffed in the chest area for humorous effect) and a white, nurse-type apron with a large breast pocket. She takes quite a few items from this pocket, so it needs an extra large inside flap sewn at the back. A watch hangs beside the pocket. A huge, ginger fright wig would be a good idea, with a tiny nurse's cap perched on the top. She should wear crazily-patterned tights and big boots. Use plenty of rouge and bright red lipstick for comical effect.

# Costume

### Prince Valentine

Whether Valentine is played by a boy or girl, he should be extremely over the top, eg, dressed from top to toe in pink, trimmed with silver, or wearing a belted tunic adorned with a red heart. The rest of his outfit could consist of a short cloak, the usual leggings/tights combination, beribboned shoes and a hat with a jaunty feather, and maybe a flowing blonde wig. He carries a sword and a pink heart shaped shield, (backed with foil, so that it doubles as a mirror).

### The Guards

The guards can wear plain tunics with breastplates on the top. These can be made from a rectangle of corrugated cardboard (100cm long by 35cm wide), sprayed silver. The ridges should run across the width. Remove a circle of cardboard (18cm in diameter) from the middle of the rectangle, to make the opening for the head. You can make helmets using papier mâché moulded onto balloons. When dry, spray silver. Each guard carries a sword.

### The Gardeners

Belted tunics, track suit bottoms tucked into boots and straw hats should suffice. One or two could carry shears or watering cans.

### The Villagers

Their costumes should be as varied as possible and can be designed to make use of the clothes you have available, eg farmers, shepherds, urchins, etc. The females can wear skirts, shawls and headscarves or mob caps.

### The Kitchen Staff

Tunics and rolled-up leggings for the boys, simple skirts and blouses for the girls, plus aprons and mob caps.

### The Spiders

Black or brown leotards and tights or leggings provide the basis for the Spiders' costumes. Each spider can wear a brown or black stocking over their head with a hole cut out for the face. Extra legs can be made from old black or brown tights and stockings, stuffed with rags or newspaper to give them substance, and attached to a neckband made from matching material.

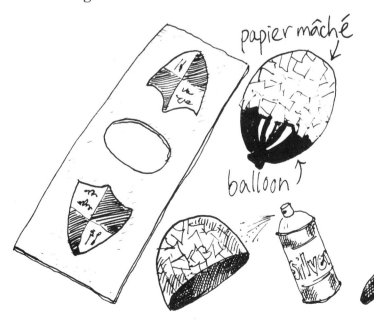

papier mâché

balloon

silver

'Cobwebs' for draping over the sleepers in Act 2, scene 3 can be made from circular pieces of white net or muslin with the cobwebs drawn on in black felt pen.

# Music

The eleven songs in the play have been written to seven well-known tunes. The actors on stage are required to sing the songs whilst remaining in character, which can be very intimidating. The solution is to have a choir. This will take the pressure off the actors and allow a great many more children to play an active part. Of course, if Nightshade, Nursey or Beauty are confident singers, encourage them to sing solo, but I strongly suggest that you use a choir to lead the rest of the songs, so that the rafters will really ring.

The songs can be accompanied on keyboard, piano or guitar. If you have an established school orchestra, a recorder group or a staff member who used to play the bassoon, this is a perfect opportunity to make use of their talents.

## Dances

The Spider dance occurs at the beginning of Act 2, scene 3. The spiders can creep onto the stage from all different directions, including the aisle. (*The Hall Of The Mountain King* from Peer Gynt would be a suitably ominous accompaniment.) Once on stage, they perform a dance in which they weave in between the frozen 'sleepers', as they 'spin their webs'. As they dance, they drape the sleepers (and the prepared feast) with cobwebs. The effect should be highly sinister.

There could also be an opportunity for some country dancing at the end of the Prologue, where the villagers are celebrating the news of the royal baby.

# Sound Effects

**Thunder**  This can be achieved by shaking sheets of flexible cardboard. Ominous minor chords played on the piano would add to the effect.

**Church bells**  A recording would be the most effective, fading away in volume to allow the Town Crier to begin his first speech.

**Knock on the door**  Rap a block of wood on a hard surface.

**Fanfare**  If there is a trumpet player in the orchestra, this is his/her big moment. If not, it would be quite fun to use a recording of a fanfare played by a great many trumpets. This would provide a moment of comic relief as the Footman lowers his solitary trumpet and stares into it in surprise and disbelief.

**Clocks**  Wood blocks would work well.

# Final Word

Finally – don't get too frazzled. It'll be hard work and you may well have a few more grey hairs to show by opening night, but just wait until you see their shining little faces at the end of the performance. I promise it'll be worth it.

# BRIAN LARA
## The Story of a Record-Breaking Year

### Jack Bannister

# Jack Bannister

Jack Bannister is, perhaps more than any other writer and broadcaster, the cricketer's choice. As a writer on the genius of Brain Lara, there is nobody better qualified. Jack has all the necessary attributes: a deep understanding of cricket, an enthusiasm for the game that he shares with his subject and a natural gift for writing.

Jack's knowledge stems from a lifetime of both playing and reporting. His playing career, beginning in 1969, spanned nineteen seasons with Warwickshire for whom he took over 1000 wickets. Writing and broadcasting followed, first as a journalist with the *Birmingham Post*, for whom he still writes, later as a commentator for Test Match Special and, currently, with BBC TV. His work has taken him on nine England tours and to over 125 Tests. Since retiring from playing Jack has also helped numerous youngsters with their game and was, for twenty years, the Secretary of the Cricketers' Association.

His admiration of Brian Lara started when he saw the young West Indian begin his international career; that admiration has now grown deeper, fostered by the hours Jack has spent watching Lara with both Warwickshire and the West Indies. His writing on Lara typifies the Bannister style. It contains insights based on experience, is clear in explanation, modest in tone and, most importantly of all, enthusiastic about every aspect of his subject.

First published 1994

1 3 5 7 9 10 8 6 4 2

First published in the United Kingdom in 1994 by
Stanley Paul
Random House, 20 Vauxhall Bridge Road,
London SW1V 2SA

Random House Australia (Pty) Limited
20 Alfred Street, Milsons Point, Sydney,
New South Wales 2061, Australia

Random House New Zealand Limited
18 Poland Road, Glenfield, Auckland 10, New Zealand

Random House South Africa (Pty) Limited
PO Box 337, Bergvlei, South Africa

Random House UK Limited Reg. No. 954009

A CIP catalogue record for this book is available
from the British Library

Typeset by SX Composing Ltd, Rayleigh, Essex

Design/make-up on Apple Macintosh by Roger Walker

Printed and bound in Great Britain
by Scotprint Ltd, Musselburgh .

ISBN 0 09 180672 0

# Contents

# THE EARLY DAYS

B rian Lara was born on 2 May, 1969, in the village of Cantaro in the Santa Cruz valley, north of Port-of-Spain on the lush island of Trinidad. Parents Bunty and Pearl already had six sons in what is now a family of eleven, ranging in age from 45 to 23. Only one of Brian's four sisters is younger than him and, much to the displeasure of mother Pearl, he is the only unmarried member of the close-knit family. The family home is still in Mitchell Street, and family ties are so important for cricket's latest and greatest superstar that he flew home from Birmingham twice in his first six weeks with Warwickshire.

▲ A young Brian with his nephew, Marvin

Not that privacy among his own exists any more for a young man whose name is now known around the world following his prodigious batting feats in the first half of 1994 – a year he has already turned into his own personal Leap Year through the record books.

Perhaps the enormousness of his achievements for West Indies, Trinidad and Warwickshire has still to register with a man who seems incapable of a remark which could be construed as boastful or irritable. No cricketer in my lifetime has been subjected to so much media attention. No man, not even Sir Garfield Sobers at the height of his career, has had every waking moment under threat from requests to sign, talk or shake hands with someone, somewhere.

Surely no man has ever resisted so successfully the trappings of fame, including the mysterious world of agents, contracts and megadeals which have already guaranteed him the status of a millionaire before his 26th birthday. He travels free, thanks to domestic airlines, following his record-breaking 375 in Antigua. He lives free, certainly in Birmingham, in accommodation provided by Warwickshire, which is far from being a bachelor flat.

His first season with Warwickshire provided many temptations, including the easily justifiable one of charging a few hundred pounds

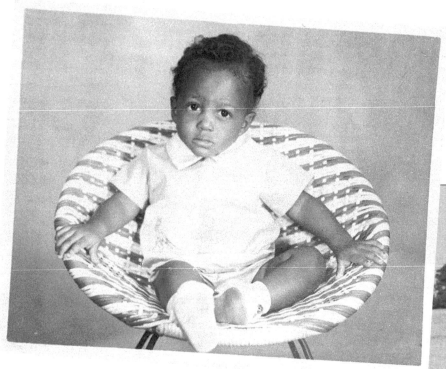

Brian Lara – aged one

... and aged twelve

here, a few there, for personal appearances. He resisted them all, and so far, under high-quality management, blessed with an expertise that combines a maximum exploitation of his name with an instinctive awareness of what best suits his image, he has walked the tightrope over the minefield of cheap glitz which usually swallows the unwary newcomer to fame.

As his surrogate father, former West Indies batsman Joey Carew, says, 'It is sometimes hard to remember he is only 25, but I don't think he will end up like that English footballer, the one who keeps injuring his leg.'

All a far cry from his early days when, as a tiny member – he is even now slightly under five and a half feet tall – of a big family, rough edges rarely developed in the inevitable rough and tumble atmosphere of such a large household. Father Bunty had little interest in cricket – until Brian was six and took his first step to cricketing fame, thanks to elder sister Agnes Cyrus.

She it was who spotted a local advertisement asking for youngsters who were interested in cricket coaching at the Harvard clinic. Agnes never forgot that Rudolph, an elder brother of Brian, made him a wooden bat when he was only three. 'He would play about hitting marbles and fruit, and he soon learned all the strokes. When I saw the advert, I bought him a little green cap, a proper bat and some white clothes and took him down

for the first two Sundays. It was then my father took over, and for the rest of his life, never missed anything Brian did at cricket. Matches, even practices, he would always be there, because he knew that Brian was destined for great things. Within a year of starting at the clinic, Brian told me that he wanted to be the world's greatest cricketer, and already the game was his whole life. When he wasn't playing, he would sit down with a piece of paper and work out fielding positions.'

**With father, Bunty**

Father Bunty was to see his son grow up into a prodigy which soon had former players, including Sobers, forecasting that a genius was about to enter the world of cricket. He watched him stride through every representative level from schoolboy, to youth, to first-class cricket for Trinidad, right to the brink of his first Test cap.

But only to the brink because, after surviving five heart attacks over the years, Bunty suffered a sixth and fatal one during the second Test in Trinidad against Pakistan on 16 April, 1988, when Brian was the appointed 12th man. He had yet to win his first full cap, which came two and a half years later in Lahore against Pakistan.

Bunty's influence on Brian was enormous, as Carew, now aged 56 and a senior official of the Queen's Park Cricket Club, appreciates. 'Bunty was a great force in Brian's upbringing. Brian might have been a bit spoiled as the youngest boy but, although his father was not a cricketer, it seemed even more important for a son to know his old man was interested, than if he had been able to coach him. When he died, there was a huge turn-out for the funeral, and the entire West Indies team went. Brian has never really talked to me about his father's death and I never saw him cry, but he loved him so much.'

Carew and his two sons had always been close to Brian, and those ties were strengthened still further after Bunty's death.

Back in the early days at Harvard, Brian spent six years under the instruction of Hugo Day, now aged 76, who rates the youngster as the most talented boy he has ever seen, even though only friendly cricket was available until he was accepted by Fatima College, one of Trinidad's best grammar schools. Acceptance was not straightforward because of marginal entrance examination results, and he nearly went to another school – until principal Mervyn Moore realised he was a cricketer.

'When Brian came here, he was so small, and that used to frustrate him at times, but we soon knew that we had a great little batsman playing for us. We have an Under-14 Giants League and he dominated it. He was marvellous at pass-out, where there is no wicket but you are out if you miss the ball. He would be in there all day.'

Another teacher, Harry Ramdass, ran the Under-14 team and remembers well how Brian developed with him. 'He struggled a bit at the start because he was playing against bigger and taller boys. Yet he never flinched and soon became a match-winner. I remember one match against St Anthony's School when we were in real trouble. Brian took over, counted the balls in such a mature way to keep the strike and always knew where the fielders were. We won the match and their coach thought it was a fluke at first, but then realised that Brian was planning it all and said he had never seen anything like it before.

'As teachers and coaches, we might point out a couple of things, but Brian was always his own hardest critic. He would think about every dismissal, and if he kept getting out to a particular stroke, he would tie a ball on a string to the net so that it would come from the problem angle, and he would hit them for hours until he had mastered the weakness.'

As Lara moved up the age scale, other coaches came under his spell as much as he with them. Francisco Garcia was the coach of the Under-16 team, and still drools about the pleasure he got from watching such an exceptional talent develop. 'I never really had to coach him, and it was just a joy to umpire and watch him bat. The thing that impressed me most was that he never seemed to hit the ball hard to the boundary – he just stroked it and it was sheer delight to watch. As for practice, he would practise at every opportunity with anything he could lay his hands on.

'I remember reading that Bradman would use a stump and a golf ball, and that Sobers would use a stump and a tennis ball. I don't know if that was true, but I do know that I often saw Brian use a ruler and a marble. [Elder brothers Michael and Winston also remember Brian's youthful wizardry with a marble. He would hit a large marble against the garage wall using a broom handle and would, single-handed, hold his own England versus West Indies Test matches. He would bat all four innings for both sides by throwing a marble in the air and hitting it. If he missed one, that would count as a wicket, but those Tests used to go on for days.] But it was not just the fact that his batting was so brilliant. He also had a perfect temperament, and never seemed to raise his voice. And something else. He never forgets us here. He always comes back to say hello, because he never forgets

▲ A typical flashing square cover drive during an innings of 160 for Trinidad v Guyana in the Youth Championship held in Barbados in 1988

his roots. That is why he finds it so easy to relax with us, and I don't think he will ever change.'

Mervyn Moore agrees with all that, and more. 'We took a team to Barbados for a tournament involving schools from the West Indies, Canada and England. We weren't very strong, but Brian really motivated the boys and found a way to get the best out of each of them. The good thing about him is that, although he is fiercely competitive, he never shouts. He has this calm authority which everyone responds to, and he always seems to be smiling.'

This was the first time that Sobers had seen Lara, now 17, and told Moore that 'He has the greatest talent I have seen for a long time.' That talent was quickly to bring him two hundreds in the Northern Telecom youth championships in Jamaica, and an entry into first-class cricket, which seemed inevitable to all who had seen him through his early teens, was not to be delayed much longer.

It came in January 1988 for Trinidad against the Leeward Islands, with his second game three weeks later against the might of Barbados, setting him on the road to greatness.

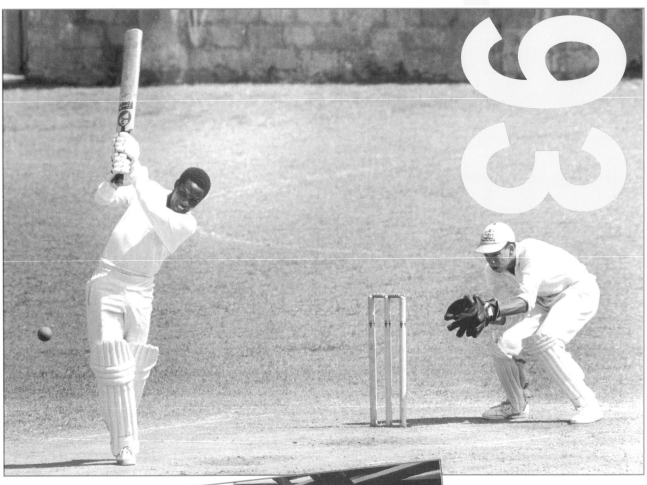

▲ On his way to an innings of 193 for Trinidad v Jamaica in the Northern Telecom Youth Championship

◀ Brian Lara flanked by the President of the Northern Telecom (Cola) Corporation, Emile Gratton, and Sir Clyde Walcott, now Chairman of the ICC. The occasion was a schools tournament in Barbados in 1988, involving teams from the West Indies, Canada and England

# FIRST-CLASS CAREER

UP TO BARBADOS TEST, APRIL 1994

B rian's second first-class game for Trinidad against Barbados provided a significant signpost for the future. Small in stature Lara may have been but, when he walked in to bat at the Queen's Park Oval at the beginning of February 1988, a big performance was needed, because his side was 14 for two and Joel Garner and Malcolm Marshall were rampant.

The reputation of the little left-hander had grown considerably in the previous year. In the Northern Telecom youth championships in Jamaica, he aggregated 498 runs, beating the previous record of 480 held by Carl Hooper, and his small frame had now developed some of the power missing the previous year when he found it difficult to hit boundaries at that level.

As captain of his island's youth team, he was just as pleased with the fact that his side was voted the most sportsmanlike as he was at winning the trophy – not a bad double to go with his record aggregate and being voted the best player.

That was in July 1987. Now, six months later, the serious stuff started, and Lara actually seemed to relish taking on two of his country's all-time great bowlers. He batted for just 11 minutes short of six hours and scored 92 out of a total of 292. Marshall was impressed, although he still thought there was room for more power. 'He must put on a bit of size.'

Garner finally dismissed him, but he was now on his way. Next month he led his national youth team in Australia in the first Youth Cup, in which his two hundreds failed to get his side to the final. On his return to the Caribbean, he was made captain of the Under-23 team against Pakistan, even though he was the youngest player in the side.

He was now pushing hard for a full Test cap, and he regrets that he was only 12th man at the Queen's Park Oval, when father Bunty died on the third day of the Test match, only a week after he had watched son Brian lead the Under-23 team at Castries.

Brian was devastated, and left the Test match immediately. His grief remained private, but he went out of his way six years later to pay public respect to a devoted man who had lavished so much time

12 BRIAN LARA: THE STORY OF A RECORD-BREAKING YEAR

The end of Lara's courageous 92 in the Red Stripe match v Barbados in Trinidad, February 1988. Joel Garner has him lbw, eight runs short of a hundred in his second first-class game

on his youngest son. After his 375 in Antigua, Lara chose his words carefully. 'It is only natural that I should want to dedicate this special innings to him. You see, my father really believed in me and always told me that one day I was going to do just this. I remember him saying that achieving anything great would not be possible without dedication, discipline and determination. Our relationship was what every young boy should have with his father, and such bonds are critical for the youth of Trinidad and Tobago these days.' Remarkably mature sentiments for a 24-year-old.

In 1989, he was picked for all three representative sides against India, the Under-23s, the President's XI and the Board XI. He hit a

A leg glance during his innings for the President's XI v India in Barbados, March 1989

magnificent 182 as captain of the Under-23s, with 90 in boundaries to show that, as requested by Marshall, he had 'put on a bit of size'. His golden season at the age of 19 included a maiden Red Stripe hundred against Guyana, a top aggregate of 336 for Trinidad in the competition, and an appointment as captain of West Indies 'B' team to tour Zimbabwe later that year. Considering that he was picked above men with full Test experience such as Carl Hooper, Patrick Patterson and Tony Gray, it was clear that the authorities had quickly appreciated personal qualities above and beyond his glittering batting skills.

He led his side well, and they won two of the three four-day games against Zimbabwe, as well as taking the one-day series 3–1, and his top score was 145 in the first drawn four-day game.

He was such a natural leader it was no surprise when, on return from the 'B' tour, he was appointed captain of Trinidad to become, at the age of 20, the youngest captain in the history of the tournament. What was a surprise was that his side finished bottom, and that his own batting form was moderate, with only 178 from eight innings, and he did not reach fifty once.

The high spot of that 1989–90 domestic season was the first glimpse for the England party and journalists of the man who was to thrill the world four years later. He scored 134 for the Board President's XI at Pointe-à-Pierre, a ground set in the not exactly picturesque middle of an oil refinery in Trinidad.

England's first sight of Lara in Guaracarra, Pointe-à-Pierre, Trinidad, where he hit 134. These three pictures show the flourish of a leg-side whip, a balanced cut and a sweep

**Not quite the Parks or Chesterfield** ▶

**The stand at Pointe-à-Pierre. Waiting for history to beckon** ▶

None of us could fail to be impressed by the grace and power of a left-hander who more than justified all the boasts made about him by the locals. His runs came out of a total of 294 and the next highest score was by his captain, Gus Logie. He is no slouch with the bat, but his 40 came out of a spectacular partnership for the fourth wicket of 131, and the exceptional promise of Lara was there for all to see.

The West Indies selectors saw it and included him in the squad for the infamous time-wasting third Test the following week, but again relegated him to 12th man. That first cap was tantalisingly close, yet would still be delayed for a further eight months.

The tour of Pakistan was short but sweet for Lara. After scoring 11 in the first one-day international, he was dropped for the next two, and even his 139 against a Combined XI would not have earned his first cap, but for a hand injury to Carlisle Best. Ironically, it was Best who, five years earlier, presented the then 16-year-old Lara with a bat which he took to India with the Trinidad and Tobago secondary schools team, and Lara has never forgotten it.

▲ **Three years later at St Johns, Lara and Chanderpaul walk out to bat with Lara 320 not out**

▲ Lara won his first cap for the third Test against Pakistan in Lahore, December 1990, (back row, far right)

Nor has he forgotten that Logie also gave him a bat in his early years, because the equally diminutive Trinidadian was one of his three boyhood idols. The first was Colin Cowdrey, whom Brian first saw when he was only five and promptly co-opted father, godfather and brothers to bowl at home to him in an attempt to master the strokes he saw from Cowdrey. English cricket might owe its most recent Knight a debt, but current England bowlers might wish Cowdrey had not proved to be such an inspiration.

Roy Fredericks was the other hero, mainly because he was left-handed, with Bunty even having to buy Brian a white shirt with long sleeves which buttoned at the wrist so he could look like Fredericks.

Lara may not have scored heavily in his first Test, but his first innings 44 helped to steady a side in trouble on the first day at 37 for three, with Gordon Greenidge, Desmond Haynes and Richie Richardson all gone – the first two to Imran Khan, while Wasim Akram had Richardson lbw. Together with Hooper, he batted for two and a half hours to share a fourth wicket partnership of 95. The Lara bandwagon had started to roll.

Not at home though, because on returning from Lahore, he found he had been replaced by Gus Logie as captain of Trinidad, apparently

# BOYHOOD HEROES:

◀ Gus Logie during the West Indies tour of England, 1991

Roy Fredericks ▶ during the second Test v England at Lord's, 1976

◀ Sir Colin Cowdrey, England captain and opener, seen here during his fine innings of 155 in the fifth Test v Australia, August 1960

▲ **Lara taking a spectacular catch to dismiss Barbados captain Roland Holder in a Red Stripe match, Barbados, January 1991**

because of fears that his batting had been affected the previous season. His reply could be said by the authorities to have proved the point, because he set a new Red Stripe record with 627 runs, despite which he was not selected for any of the five Tests in the acrimonious series against Australia.

His domestic record was overtaken within a week by Desmond Haynes, but nothing was more certain than that the record would revert to Lara, as it did three seasons later.

He was selected for the 1991 tour of England but despite poor returns from Logie, Hooper and Simmons – 572 runs between the trio in 22 completed Test innings – he still could not force his way into a batting line-up that was both ageing and creaking. He was unlucky to injure an ankle during practice for the fourth Test at Edgbaston, otherwise he would have played at the Oval, but his non-selection earlier bordered on the incomprehensible.

He averaged only 28.41 in the eight first-class matches he played on the tour but, as subsequent events proved, it was a stubborn selection policy to deny him experience until the retirement from international cricket at the end of that tour by Viv Richards.

◀ **The 600 club – Brian Lara and Desmond Haynes in 1991. Lara became the first West Indies batsman to score over 600 runs in a season. Desmond Haynes broke that record the week after**

◀ **Lara at Arundel, May 1991**

Lara facing Ian Botham at
Worcester, May 1991

When his career is finally assessed, the curio will be the 18-month
gap between his first and second Test caps. A minor consolation was
a string of one-day internationals, including the 1992 World Cup in
Australia and New Zealand. That tournament finally confirmed his
arrival, with 174 of his 333 runs in eight games coming in boundaries.
He averaged 47.57 and scored at a staggering rate of 81 runs per 100
balls – around five runs per over. This statistic was the first hard evidence of a natural scoring rate in all cricket that was to become a
trademark unique in the modern game.

▲ World Series cricket. Australia v West Indies, January 1992

▶ West Indies v Pakistan, Melbourne, 23 February, 1992. Brian Lara during his innings of 88. Wicket-keeper Moin Khan watches. Lara retired hurt and the West Indies went on to score 221 and won by ten wickets

He returned to the Caribbean to play his second Test in the one-off match against South Africa, and his second innings of 64 in a relatively low-scoring game was bedevilled by controversy. When 50, he trod on his stumps as television replays clearly showed, but neither umpire Archer nor umpire Bucknor felt able to give him out, despite the grounded bail. As the picture on page 31 shows, he did the same again two years later when he played the hook from Chris Lewis that took him from 365 to 369.

# BARBADOS 1992

▶ West Indies v South Africa, Barbados, 1992. Lara trod on his stumps, but unsighted and bemused umpire Steve Bucknor gave him not out. This incident led to the use of television replays

▼ The two teams from that historic test. Lara is third from left, back row

SIR GARFIELD SOBERS PAVILION

With great players, it is just a matter of when, not if, they produce an innings of a lifetime. Sobers took four years from debut before his record unbeaten 365 at Kingston against Pakistan. For Lara, it took five Tests and 25 months. He limbered up with half centuries in the first two Tests against Australia in December 1992 in Brisbane and Melbourne, but what a New Year present he bequeathed to cricket in Sydney!

He still rates his 277 as the best innings he has ever played, because of the state of the match – 31 for two when he went in – and the quality of an attack which included McDermott, Hughes and Warne. In just under eight hours, he faced only 372 balls – a personal

◀ Australia v West Indies, third Test, Sydney, 2-6 January, 1993. Brian Lara during his innings of 277. Note the opening of the face of the bat

◀ Same game – Lara is run out by Ian Healy after scoring 277. Damien Martyn was the fielder and Carl Hooper was Lara's partner

▼ Fourth Test, Adelaide, 23-27 January, 1993. Lara and Ian Bishop celebrate a West Indies victory by one run

◀ The West Indies celebrate victory in the fifth Test and the series, Perth, 30 January to 3 February, 1993

▶ A whipped stroke through mid-wicket against Pakistan in April 1993

rate of around 4.5 runs per six balls faced – in a performance which Rohan Kanhai described as 'one of the best innings I have ever seen'. Wisden said that the innings changed the course of, not only the match, but the series which was slipping away after Australia won the previous Test in Melbourne.

Together with skipper Richie Richardson, he shared in a third-wicket partnership of 293 which prompted this praise from his captain, whose 109 was his 15th hundred for West Indies and his eighth against Australia. Asked about his own innings, Richardson said, 'I can hardly remember it. It was difficult playing and being a spectator at the same time.'

When Lara was finally run out, his 277 was the third highest-ever score against Australia behind Len Hutton's 364 and Reg 'Tip' Foster's 287. His runs came out of 450 scored while he was at the crease and, on average, he outscored his three partners, Richardson, Arthurton and Hooper by two to one.

Finally, at the age of 23, Lara had arrived on the centre stage on which he was to stagger the world in the next 18 months. More hundreds were rattled off later in the year but, frustratingly for everyone, they were all in limited-overs cricket, and he started the 1994 home season with only one hundred in 11 Tests. Asked what his goals were for the year, he said 'To get a few centuries, maybe a double and even

# W E S T
# I N D I E S

◄ Second one-day international, Jamaica, 26 February 1994. Lara's individual leg-side pull with the right foot well off the ground

◄ West Indies v England, first Test, Jamaica, 19-24 February 1994. Lara is bowled behind his legs by Hick for 83

◄ A rash costly stroke against Caddick off the penultimate ball of the fourth day of the Jamaica Test when eight were needed for victory

▶ Second Test, Guyana, 17-22 March, 1994. Lara during his innings of 167. Jack Russell says, 'Please may we have our ball back?'

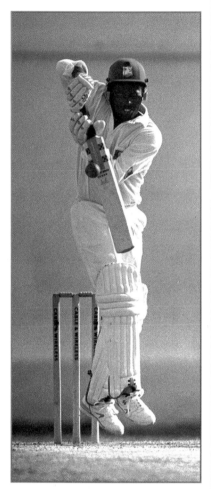

▲ Note how the face of the bat is closing for a late-adjusted leg glance

▶ Graham Thorpe watches a happy Lara and Adams during the Guyana Test, March 1994

a triple.' Halfway through the year, he had a single, and a triple for his country, two singles and a double for Trinidad, and six singles and a quintuple for Warwickshire.

In the Red Stripe tournament, he scored a new record aggregate of 715, with no other batsman in the tournament reaching 500. Just as pleasing to him was his reinstatement as captain of Trinidad, with all those runs making a nonsense of any theory that the extra responsibility inhibits his batting.

With his record domestic season out of the way, he could concentrate on England, and he gave them a taste with 167 in the second Test in Georgetown. He hit 25 fours and, again, a total of 210 balls faced gave him a personal run-rate of nearly five runs per over faced.

Curtly Ambrose's historic spell on the fourth evening wrapped up the win, and so to Barbados where England also claimed a piece of

history by winning only the second Test against the West Indies at Bridgetown in nearly 60 years. Lara scored 64 in the second innings, but was criticised for a rash-looking dismissal on the final day.

Whether or not the comments stung, and whether they were justified is now washed away by the astonishing events in Antigua five days later. Back-to-back Tests often produce an anticlimax – viz. South Africa against Australia in Durban three weeks earlier – but Lara flew into Antigua with something quite different in mind.

▲ **Not a tall man, Lara often makes extra height in this unorthodox manner against Lewis**

◀ **Lara has been hit in the eye while fielding. A worried Ambrose calls the medics**

# THE INNINGS

S eldom, if ever, has one stroke in cricket meant so much to one man, as Brian Lara's hook for four off Chris Lewis at 11.46 a.m. on Monday, 18 April. Had the bail he dislodged in making the stroke, fallen to the floor, he would have remained level with Sir Gary Sobers in what would have been the most unlikely dead-heat in sporting history.

History was thus made at the Recreation Ground in St Johns, as often happens, only by a fractional twist of the law of gravity, and so Lara was able to enjoy a much better night's sleep than the previous one, when he tossed and turned from 4 a.m. onwards.

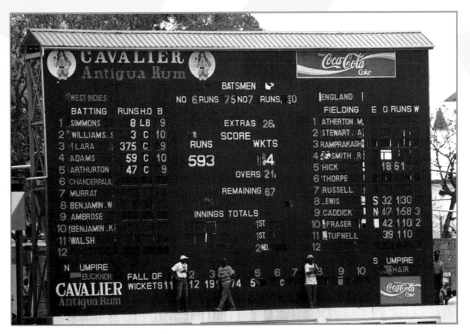

Would he or wouldn't he be in a position to accept the baton marked 'Record Test Score'? Only eight men had earned the right to hold it, starting with Charles Bannerman in 1877, passing on through the years to Billy Murdoch, Reginald 'Tip' Foster, Andy Sandham, Don Bradman, Walter Hammond, Len Hutton and Sobers.

Four Englishmen, three Australians and a West Indian. Lara hardly dared think about becoming the ninth man to carry the baton in 117 years, especially as the first seven men held it for 81 years between them, with Foster's 27 years the longest period of ownership until Sobers.

He had won it 36 years earlier, and the possibility of him handing it over made sleep impossible.

Early dawn is an unforgiving time for the worried mind – even one which could look back on an overnight, unbeaten score of 320. Most cricketers profess to be ignorant and uncaring of records, but the truth is usually different. As with Lara who, in his room at the

1994

◀ Triumph and relief that the record and the bails are intact. St Johns, 18 April, 1994

▼ Brian Lara plays the stroke that took him past Sobers' Test batting record. Note the bail on the left. Lara dislodged his off bail in hitting the record-breaking four off Lewis, but it did not fall to the ground

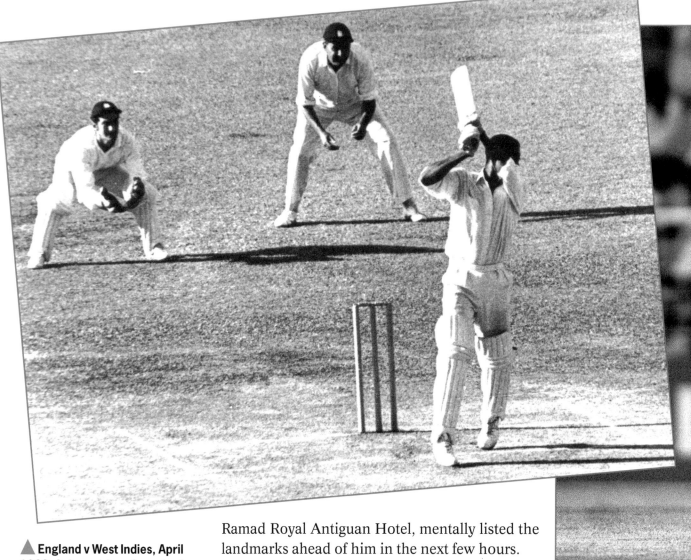

England v West Indies, April 1968. Sobers drives Snow for four during his innings of 95 not out. Alan Knott and Colin Cowdrey wait in vain

Ramad Royal Antiguan Hotel, mentally listed the landmarks ahead of him in the next few hours.

The first run of the morning would maintain a Test average of 63, and the first boundary would take him past 750 runs for the series. Graham Gooch's 333 was 13 runs away, and he could then knock off Bradman, Hammond and Hanif Mohammad with one boundary. Left then would be Hutton and Sobers – the latter on the top of the mountain alongside the flag marked '365' which had flown proudly for 36 years.

When Lara arrived at the ground, the tension-filled atmosphere was winding up to a drum-tight level. Crowds poured in from 8 a.m. onwards. Radio and television stations were full of it. Desmond Haynes, captain in Lara's first Test in Lahore, and out of the fifth Test with an injured finger, flew back from Barbados to give moral support, and Trinidad and Tobago's Minister of Sport, Jean Pierre, was also there.

But for rain on the second day which caused Lara to restart his innings three extra times, his date with destiny would have been kept, but the weather gods are no respecters of sport. They took 23 overs

out of the day but, although they relented on the third morning, they cost him most of his sleep during Sunday night.

He started edgily, and soon had the third new ball to deal with after two overs. His first stroke against it lobbed one from Andrew Caddick over cover for his 40th and least convincing four. He then played and missed at one from Angus Fraser, which brought this long-suffering comment: 'I don't suppose I can call you a lucky bugger when you're 340.'

The world watched and waited ... and gasped as, three times in one over from

▲ Singing in the rain

◄ Another fierce pull during his 375

# WEST INDIES

1994

▲ Delicate adjustment for a cut

▶ A rare misjudgement off Caddick during Lara's 375

Lewis, he took on a fielder with the ball in his hand for a second run. Now he was 357. He wafted and missed a drive in Lewis's next over, and promptly got a steadying rebuke from his 19-year-old partner, Shivnarine Chanderpaul. Around the Caribbean and in many other parts of the world, the rest of life stood still. His family were crowded

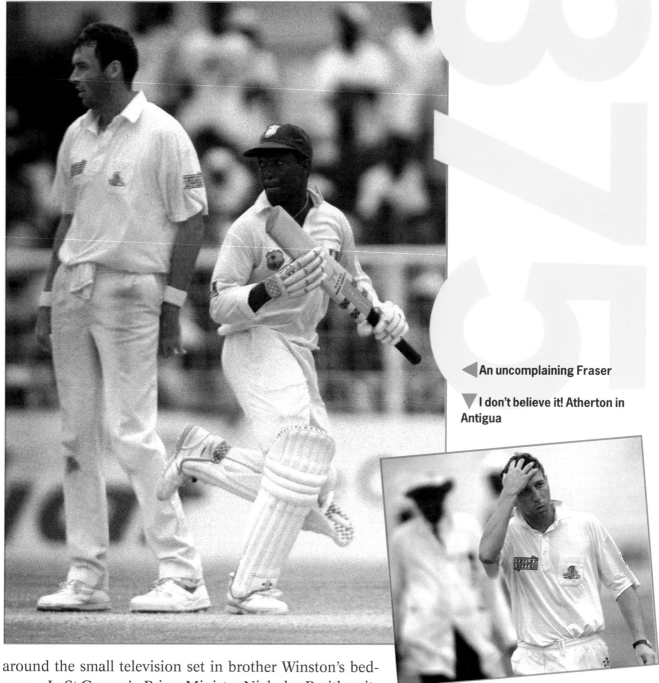

◀ **An uncomplaining Fraser**

▼ **I don't believe it! Atherton in Antigua**

around the small television set in brother Winston's bed-room. In St George's, Prime Minister Nicholas Braithwaite adjourned a sitting of the Grenada cabinet. Even law and order had to wait in Kingston, where an important High Court Case was halted in St Vincent.

In England, rush-hour workers and shoppers, ready to head home at 5 p.m. local time, had a free view on television sets in shop windows, and the usual lengthy Chairman's annual lunch at Edgbaston looked like merging into dinner.

An extra-cover four off Caddick took Lara from 361 past Hutton and level with the watching Sobers. Atherton, quite properly, tried to

▶ The great celebration at St Johns, Antigua, after Lara beat the 365 of Sobers

▶ Lara congratulated by former Captain Vivian Richards. Winston Benjamin looks on

turn the screw. A fielding circle was meticulously posted to try to prevent a single, but true men of destiny do not creep over the finishing line.

They finish with a flourish, and so it was this time. He swivelled, he lashed … and he exulted once he knew that his brush with the off stump was not terminal. The emotional release for everyone was immense and draining. Spectators jumped and waved in the West Indies Oil Company Stand, as the ghetto-blasters of Chickie's Disco blared out.

The two main cheer-leaders were called Gravy and Mayfield, with the first-named dressed as Santa Claus, and they were ecstatic. As Lara was engulfed, Mayfield symbolically broke his own records – two L.P.s he had brought along for the occasion – and the only worried people on the ground were the police who, somehow, had to get Sobers and Lara together, away from the madding crowd.

From the record-sealing boundary until Lara faced another ball

▲▲ 'Take the baton with my blessing.' Sir Garfield Sobers embraces Lara at the Recreation Ground, after the boundary which took Lara from 365 to 369

▲ Happiness is a world record. Sobers and Lara

◀ Fifth Test, Antigua, 16-21 April, 1994. Mayfield symbolically breaking a record of his own

took more than five minutes while the Prince was crowned King, with his coronation only the start of 10 days of celebration that no other cricketer has ever experienced.

Everyone who was there, and thousands who were not but will claim they were in years to come, have had their say about the innings, and more than one person echoes the view of the senior commentator in the Caribbean, Tony Cozier.

At the end of the first day when Lara was 164 not out, he wrote, 'The £50,000 sterling for the first batsman to score a double-hundred in the series, is all but in his bank account. By tea-time this afternoon, the consideration might well be directed to a less lucrative, but far more prestigious prize. Sir Gary Sobers' Test record of 365. On yesterday's evidence, it is not a ridiculous thought, and Sir Gary is here to follow his successor's progress.

▲ Lara and Arthurton celebrate during the 375

▶ Lift from a fan

'I have reported dozens of innings at a similar stage, but never felt so certain that something extraordinary was developing. It was a sixth sense shared by one or two journalists in the press box.'

And by the England Captain. Atherton later agreed that the innings smacked of the inevitable.

Before Lara, only 12 scores of over 300 had been registered in Test cricket, with Bradman the only man to do it twice.

The innings statistics show that Lara faced 538 balls, batted for 12 and a half hours and hit 45 fours on a slow, coarse, long-leaf grass outfield. The bat he used was, oddly enough, one returned to him after being stolen in Port-of-Spain in February. Such was his standing on his native island, even before the 375, that, as soon as the miscreant knew the identity of his victim, he put the matter right

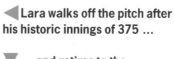

◀ Lara walks off the pitch after his historic innings of 375 ...

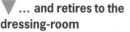

▼ ... and retires to the dressing-room

◀ Note the sparkling eyes immediately after his 375

▼ Note the tired eyes following his 501

immediately, even though it meant transporting the kit-bag to Jamaica.

Like his epic innings in Sydney 15 months earlier, Lara came in to bat with his side in trouble. This time they were 11 for one which was soon 12 for two and, with no Haynes or Richie Richardson playing because of injury, he walked proudly in to take guard as the temporarily appointed Vice-Captain.

Of the next 581 runs scored, Adams, Arthurton and Chanderpaul scored 180 from 510 balls – arguably the most staggering comparative statistic of them all.

Lara's immediate public reaction was typically low-key, full of declared intentions which were soon to be put to a test he would pass and pass again with flying colours.

'I think the public will put a lot of pressure on me and I'll have to live up to what I have done today and what I've done in the past. Just that is enough inspiration to keep going. I know that, because I have the world record, people will be expecting a lot, and I can't afford to disappoint them.'

1994

More cautiously, he said, 'There are times when I shall fail and I hope that people understand that I'm just a human being and it takes one ball to get you out. From now on, I'll be going out just to maintain what I've done today and maintain my career.'

He flew back to Trinidad after the Test ended on Thursday, 21 April, and the reception awaiting him at Piarco International airport was the start of a merry-go-round which would whirl ever faster in the months of May and June.

Prime Minister Patrick Manning was there to greet him, and the gifts started to pour in. BWIA International gave him TT$375,000 of free travel – roughly $50,000 – and a cellular telephone company gave him 375 minutes of free air time. A soap company chipped in with TT$37,500, and a free new house from the government was promised.

A street in Independence Square was renamed 'Brian Lara Promenade', and all schools were given the following day off, to watch their hero lead a motorcade tour of the island. It started in Arima in central Trinidad but, such were the crowds, his journey to the City Hall to receive the keys of the city, took more than two hours. The tour finished at the Queen's Park Oval, where happy schoolchildren had waited for more than three hours in sweltering heat.

That evening, he attended a reception at the Prime Minister's residence, and the next day, together with Sobers, was presented with the Trinity Cross, the island's highest honour. Tour followed tour,

◀ Happy families – mother and sister greeting Brian at the airport

Song and dance men – the musical celebration the evening of the 375. Viv Richards, Richie Richardson and Curtly Ambrose join in

▲ That famous kiss. Lara expresses his gratitude to the Antiguan turf

including one to his own Santa Cruz, followed by visits to the southern towns of Chaguanas and San Fernando.

That left the twin island of Tobago, with this visit delaying his return to Trinidad, causing him to miss his flight to England where he was due to arrive by Tuesday, 26 April. Seats on later planes were full, but the power of his name enabled him to arrive, finally, at Edgbaston on Wednesday, 27 April, less than 24 hours before the start of his first game since the Antigua Test match.

The world's media had now got him firmly in their sights. He dominated the sports pages in many countries, and many front pages as well. Even several editorials in British national newspapers

switched from their normal political and economic themes.

More locally, his own island's *Daily Express* ran a 24-page special 'Tribute to Brian Lara', and the *Daily Nation* of Barbados printed eight pages of stories and pictures. Jamaica's *Gleaner* was fortunate to have Tony Becker writing about Lara, because Becker was the only journalist to have seen Sobers set the then new record at Sabina Park 36 years earlier.

Most Australian newspapers used headlines referring to the picture of Lara kissing the pitch on the Recreation Ground. 'Sealed with a kiss' was the popular choice.

In India, he was given front-page prominence ahead of that country's progress in the Australasia Cup in Sharjah, and Canadian newspapers gave splash coverage to his feat for their many hundreds of thousands of West Indian immigrants.

Even America was drawn in, although newscaster Nick Charles on cable network CNN admitted that he had no idea what he was talking about after doing a voice-over on the stroke which clinched the record for his station's 'Michelin Play of the Day'.

By then Lara had learned that he had an eyesight problem. Incredible as it seems for a young man blessed with such exceptional reflexes, he suffers from pterygium, which causes a light film to spread from the corner of the eye towards the cornea.

This was diagnosed during the second Test in Georgetown, when Lara complained of irritation and itchiness in his eyes. He was told that the condition, peculiar to hot, dry countries, necessitated an operation, which would be done before he toured India with the West Indies towards the end of 1994.

What might he have achieved had he been able to see what he was doing ….

Warwickshire's signing of Brian Lara could turn out to be the most glorious fluke in the history of the club. The search for an overseas replacement for Allan Donald, who toured England with South Africa in 1994, began in mid-summer the previous year.

Knowing that their fast bowler would miss a year, the Warwickshire think-tank of Chairman M. J. K. Smith, Cricket Chairman Dennis Amiss and Director of Coaching Bob Woolmer, examined the strengths and weaknesses of the county side, and decided that they would sign a top batsman.

Various names were considered, including that of Lara, whom Woolmer had seen hit two one-day international hundreds earlier that year in South Africa. Club captain Dermot Reeve was also a fan, having seen his historic 277 for West Indies against Australia in Sydney in the 1993 New Year Test.

But the first approach was made to Lara's fellow Trinidadian, Phil Simmons, only for him to ask for a two-year contract which he was subsequently offered by Leicestershire. The Warwickshire authorities could not accede to this, because of their contractual commitment to Donald for the 1995 season, so they next turned to Australia's David Boon. By this time, leg-spinner Shane Warne was destroying England in the Ashes series, but a preliminary enquiry to him revealed it was unlikely that the Australian Board of Control would allow their spinner to play county cricket – mainly because of the amount of limited-overs cricket played.

There was no such problem with Boon, and preliminary, mutually satisfactory, discussions took place during the fifth Cornhill Test at Edgbaston. He would have been the ideal man for a side full of promising young batsmen, but which lacked a man capable of playing the sort of major innings which can influence a game. Smith, Amiss and Woolmer were sold, but Reeve was not. He now believed that the side's best interests would be served by an all-rounder, and he was keen to sign the Indian Test cricketer, Manoj Prabhakar.

The Club's three senior cricket officers tried hard to change Reeve's mind, but he was adamant and, to the credit of the authorities, they gave way on the basis that it is little use acquiring a guard dog and then barking for him.

Prabhakar visited Edgbaston before the end of the 1993 season and signed a contract for 1994.

By the following January, Mike Smith was on managerial duty with England in the West Indies, Woolmer was similarly engaged with Boland in South Africa and Reeve was in Hong Kong, coaching the national side prior to their participation in the International Cricket Council's mini-World Cup to be held the following month in Kenya.

The first note of disquiet was when Prabhakar was forced to return home from India's tour of New Zealand in February, and the alarm bells started to ring at Edgbaston. Amiss was appointed in March to the post of Chief Executive in succession to the late David Heath, and the first potato handed to him was a hot one.

He was asked to ascertain the fitness of Prabhakar, with the matter now of the utmost urgency with the start of the new county season only a few weeks away. The Indian insisted he would be fully fit by mid-April, but he was ordered to present himself in Birmingham together with medical certificates, before the end of March. Meanwhile, Mike Smith was asked by the committee to approach Brian Lara, which he did after receiving permission from West Indies officials, Chief Executive Steve Camacho, and Team Manager Rohan Kanhai, himself a former Warwickshire batsman.

Smith spoke to Lara during the second Test in Guyana in mid-March on an either-or basis and, once his keenness to play county cricket was communicated to Edgbaston, events moved at breakneck speed. Prabhakar, albeit reluctantly, came to see Amiss before the end of March, and the club's medical advisers expressed the view that the all-rounder's ankle would not stand up to the strain of a full English county season. An agreed compensation freed both parties from their agreement, and a one-year contract was quickly hammered out between Amiss, on behalf of his Committee, and Jonathan Barnett,

▲ Warwickshire's two star overseas players, Lara and Allan Donald, watch the successful outcome of the bowl-out against Kent in the Benson & Hedges quarter-final on 25 May, 1994. Six weeks later Lara won a winner's medal at Lord's

who was acting in a managerial capacity for Lara. Barnett is a well established figure in the entrepreneurial side of sport, and other cricketers on his books include Simmons and Jimmy Adams.

Warwickshire's Vice-Chairman, Tony Cross, flew into Barbados with the contract before the start of the fourth Test on 8 April to complete a deal which, in the slow-moving waters of cricket, was akin to shooting the rapids with a ballpoint pen as an oar.

William Shakespeare was a Man of Warwickshire, and he had it about right when he wrote, 'There is a tide in the affairs of men, which, taken at the flood, leads on to fortune.'

Seldom, if ever, have the fortunes of a county cricket club received such a boost as was to happen in the next 14 days. Had the Prabhakar puzzle not been unravelled for another three weeks, Warwickshire would surely have had to pay more than the agreed £40,000 – in fact Lara might have been out of their price range.

The news of his signing was greeted with approval, but nothing more, from supporters who, in the previous 25 years had been able to watch Kanhai, Alvin Kallicharan and Lance Gibbs from the Caribbean. All was to change on Monday, 18 April, coincidentally the same day on which the Chairman's annual 'welcome back' luncheon for players, staff and local media was held at the County Ground.

Cross presided, with Smith sitting spellbound at the Recreation Ground in St Johns as Lara knocked on the door of history. His future playing colleagues, just back from a pre-season tour of Zimbabwe, roared their man on as he broke the record, and the telephones started to ring, with hundreds of people anxious to become new members at an average cost of £60 each. By the start of the season, 1000 such cheques had been banked, and the city of Birmingham breathlessly awaited Lara's arrival on Wednesday, 27 April, just six days after the end of the Antigua Test match, and 24 hours before Warwickshire's first Britannic Assurance County Championship four-day game against Glamorgan.

Amiss had shrewdly organised a press conference at the ground, and over 50 journalists and reporters for television and radio assem-

bled at 1 p.m. – only to kick their heels for over an hour. The plan was to drive him straight from touchdown at Heathrow, but a request from the High Commissioner of Trinidad to meet his island's most famous celebrity, could hardly be refused, and so the biggest little man in cricket finally walked into his future county headquarters for the first time shortly before 2 p.m.

Hardbitten hacks fired the usual questions which ranged from the banal to the loaded, but Lara never made a mistake. He was patient and courteous, but firmly resisted any attempt to get from him a cheap headline, and spotted any hand-grenade-type questions almost before they had been primed. It was as impressive a performance as any he was to achieve with the bat in the next few weeks.

▲ Which way? Lara backing up a confused Warwickshire duo, Ostler and Reeve

The only blip was when Colin Price of the *Daily Mirror* tried to present Lara with a huge celebratory cake, unaware then that Lara had signed an exclusive contract with the *Daily Mail*, whose representatives that day were Brian Scovell and Alan Fraser. They stopped pictures being taken, until Price shrewdly pointed out that their refusal to allow their man to accept the cake would make a bigger story than if he did accept it, and something resembling peace broke out. At least it did until two days later when Fraser wrote that Price had expressed the wish that Lara would get a duck – a comment the *Daily Mirror* man hotly denied making.

From Cantaro and peace and quiet, to Edgbaston and cakes and ducks – all in a fortnight in which a 24-year-old young man had turned the world of cricket upside down, and now the rest of the world was trying to do the same to his life.

The Edgbaston press box would normally have housed half a dozen journalists the following day, but Thursday, 28 April was different, with 36 media representatives there, all more anxious than the two captains about the result of the toss. Hugh Morris immediately became bottom of the popularity poll by calling correctly and deciding to bat, and distinguished writers like the *Daily Mail*'s Ian Wooldridge – three men from the *Mail* now – were reduced to logging that, at 11.20 a.m., Lara touched the ball for the first time in England, for Warwickshire, on a cold Thursday, in April ... and so on.

Slight relief came just before tea, when Reeve asked his star to bowl, but six balls for seven runs must have convinced the captain that a more rewarding return on the club's outlay would come from bat, rather than ball. The day dragged on but, even though a left-hander scored an unbeaten 109, the fact that it was Glamorgan's David Hemp who obliged, meant a wasted day for two-thirds of the press congregation – only 13 of whom would be allowed to return next day, because of the feverish impatience of their editors to place them elsewhere on the sporting merry-go-round.

What sort of state Lara was in, mentally and physically, can only be imagined. Since the end of the Antigua Test, a week before, he had been garlanded, fêted, ticker-taped and paraded around his native island. He had been bombarded with free air travel, a free house, free use of a mobile telephone, received the keys of an oil city and received Trinidad and Tobago's highest honour, the Trinity Cross, from President Noor Hassanali, as well as having a National Day of Achievement proclaimed at the same time as the National Trade Union Centre protest action was called off.

Now here he was at Edgbaston, waiting for his turn to bat to see whether the cricketing gods would exact retribution for all they had given to him in the first four months of 1994.

If the Glamorgan captain, Morris, was the most unpopular cricketer on Thursday, Warwickshire openers Dominic Ostler and Roger Twose shared that billing on Friday, 29 April, the day that was to start a run of scores for Lara, unparalleled in Warwickshire history and, mostly, in first-class cricket as well.

The young openers, 14 months younger and 12 months older than Lara respectively, put on 50 for the first wicket. Normally, home spectators would have been pleased, but there was a general air of impatience not entirely confined to the press box, rather like that in a theatre as the audience waits for the leading actor to appear.

Then it happened. Ostler's dismissal, bowled by Ottis Gibson, brought cheers all round, followed by a hush as everyone waited for their first glimpse of Lara the batsman. At 2.04 p.m., he wandered to the middle, looking even smaller than 5ft. 5in. as he took guard. Gibson against Lara. Barbados against Trinidad. The door of history opened.

▲ Lara starts his only over against Glamorgan on his debut day for Warwickshire, 28 April, 1994. Note the capped player's sweater. Lara is the only man in the club's history to be awarded his cap before debut

't's his backlift,' says David Graveney. 'It's how straight he brings the bat down,' says Hugh Morris. Warwickshire colleague, Keith Piper says, 'I remember seeing him for the first time when I toured the West Indies with Haringey College in 1987 and it was clear then that he was an exceptional player. I have never seen anyone I have batted with or kept wicket to, who opens or closes the face of the bat in mid-stroke like Brian does. That is why he has so many strokes.'

'Utter concentration is the answer,' according to Nigel Briers. Warwickshire's Director of Coaching, Bob Woolmer insists that, 'High backlift comes from a rotation of the shoulders which automatically puts his hands high.'

Mike Gatting says, 'His footwork is impeccable and he is such a watchful batsman.' Another of Lara's colleagues, Paul Smith, agrees. 'He got two beamers from Graham Rose at Taunton and watched them all the way. Most of us just instinctively duck.' John Emburey, not prone to overstatement about any cricketer, also mentions his neat footwork which 'makes him so difficult to contain. A bit short or wide and you've gone for four.'

England team manager, Keith Fletcher, says, 'He must be the world's number one, because he can destroy an attack.' Umpire John Holder believes that, 'He is improving all the time. I saw him last year in Sharjah and he was superb then. Now he is even better, and I reckon it all stems from how still he keeps his head. That gives him balance and the ability to watch the ball all the way.'

And so on ... and so on .... In his first two months in English cricket, he decimated the attacks of Glamorgan, Leicestershire, Somerset, Middlesex, Durham and Northamptonshire, with only one spell from Curtly Ambrose making him look ordinary, and won an ever-increasing army of admirers among sound judges, who do not deal readily in hyperbole.

Summarising the expressed views, it seems that his phenomenal success is based on an expansive backlift, lovely footwork, extraordinary power and placement, together with an ability to watch the ball and concentrate given to few. Genius often defies analysis. Put another way, it is difficult to describe, but instantly recognisable.

He walked in to bat at Edgbaston on Friday, 29 April, soon after lunch to face compatriot Ottis Gibson from Barbados. Expectation was sky-high. Hardened cricket reporters jabbered away as though to try to relieve a tension which was almost tangible. Either a hundred or a duck was the story … but which one would they write about?

The last ball he had faced in first-class cricket was the one from Andrew Caddick he edged to Jack Russell in Antigua. It seemed light years away, so much had happened since – yet from leaving the crease in Antigua to arriving in the middle at Edgbaston, was only, to the minute, three hours short of 11 days.

No practice, little sleep, and the handicap of how to follow a world record Test innings. All the variables of batting must have crossed even his focused mind. The unplayable ball which pitches leg stump and flicks the off bail – like the one Mike Gatting got from Shane Warne at Old Trafford. Or a bad umpiring decision. Or even a run-out in which he would be blameless. If Denis Compton could run brother Leslie out in the latter's own benefit match when the opposition was trying to give him the time-honoured single to get off the mark, anything was possible.

The Glamorgan players were wound up, and so was partner Roger Twose. How could one man deal with all this?

He started edgily, with none of the first six balls he received hitting the middle of the bat, but the seventh from Robert Croft did, and rocketed away for the first of 23 fours – 14 of which were through his favourite off-side area, either side of square point. He was away.

Not often is a journalist satisfied with his copy when he reads it a few weeks later. I am happy with this extract from my match report of that momentous day for readers of the *Birmingham Post*.

'Cricket's next millionaire played like one at Edgbaston yesterday in a staggering innings of 147. That is a score which the two Steves, Hendry and Davis, would kill for at the Crucible, but although no records came Brian Lara's way in his dazzling display, he achieved the near-impossible feat of justifying the mountain of hyperbole which has been spoken and written about him in the last two weeks.

'He came in at 2.04 p.m. to a great reception from a crowd of around 3000, and he departed to a standing ovation from a slightly larger number, with the entire Glamorgan team warmly applauding the man who had just taken them to the cleaners. His 147 came off 160 balls, and were scored out of 209 off the bat in the 165 minutes he spent partnering an admiring and unselfish Roger Twose.

'The little left-hander has the touch of genius. His pick-up is right out of the Sobers mould. High, expansive and picked up towards gully, but it is then looped round to descend ramrod straight towards the line of the ball. Just how good a runner between the wickets he is, is not clear, mainly because he only seems to score anything other than boundaries, to change ends towards the end of an over.'

He made an indirect reference to his boundary count of 104 out of 147, at a press conference at the end of the day. Asked if he was tired after such an innings, he said, 'Not really. I didn't have to run much.'

He used a brand-new bat, having decided that the one he used in Antigua was for keeping and not using. Most batsmen break their bats in before using them, but not Lara. He takes one out of the wrapping and uses it straightaway.

His captain, Dermot Reeve, was asked for his view of Lara's innings. 'He provided the best session of batting I have seen since I came to Edgbaston, and I just feel sorry for the Birmingham public that they are going to watch me after he gets out.'

As Lara walked off, the Glamorgan wicket-keeper, Colin Metson, heard one of his colleagues say, 'You do realise … none of us even managed to get a dive in.' His captain, Morris, endorsed this with the following comment to me, 'It was frightening to watch his treatment of our bowlers as soon as they were fractionally off line or length, and afterwards I realised that I couldn't see any green knees among our fielders.

'His placement was great, but he hits the ball so hard that fielders have got no chance if it is slightly wide of them. I can't see he has any weakness, and he is so run-hungry. His stamina is good, and he has such a great selection of strokes. I thought I would never see anyone better than Viv Richards, but now I'm not sure. I had seen him once before in a day–night game in Trinidad four years ago when we were on tour there, but now he is the complete batsman. He can play it to all parts, and that 147 against us was a classic.'

Thanks to Lara, Warwickshire won a match, by an innings and 103 with four hours to spare, that without him they might have lost after Glamorgan batted first and scored 365 in just over four sessions. He proved the point that in four-day cricket, one of the keys is to post big totals scored at a fast pace. That way an attack is given more time in which to take 20 wickets.

The other beneficial spin-off was the 277 scored by Twose, his first hundred for two years, and more championship runs than he managed in the whole of 1993. Twose was to be the first of his colleagues to realise that his horizons needed widening, and each of the top six local batsmen would derive great benefit in the next few weeks from watching, and batting with, a man to whom the art of batting encompassed strokes and scores they had never seen before.

Paul Smith, who partnered him at Taunton where Lara was to score his fifth successive first-class hundred, says that, 'He doesn't chat much while you are batting with him. He is easily the best player

I have ever seen, because he is so watchful and plays so straight. He is no great time-keeper as far as turning up is concerned, but I've got no problem with that, because he has showed the rest of us what can be achieved in cricket. He has mixed well with us, and when we are away, he always comes out with us. He is quiet and patient, and he has been a huge bonus for everyone at Edgbaston.'

His next game was also at Edgbaston and, astonishingly, he went one better by scoring two separate hundreds of contrasting sorts against Leicestershire. He hit 18 fours in a dazzling 106 out of his side's 254 and then, in the second innings when they could have lost after being set a victory target of 285 from 57 overs, he saved the match with a wonderful unbeaten 120 from 160 balls.

Nobody else topped 20, and his runs came out of 184 scored while he was batting. Starting with his 375 in Antigua, this gave him four hundreds in a row, and the travelling press were committed to staying with him until his golden run ended.

Taunton was the next station for the Lara Express, and the tiny press box was bursting at the seams for the four-day championship match, and the Sunday League match which was televised by the BBC. Rain washed out all Saturday and half of Sunday, but the same weather gods who delayed his record in Antigua now came to his rescue in curious fashion.

Somerset declared towards the end of the second day on Friday at 355 for nine, and Warwickshire scored 57 without loss that evening. Had either Dominic Ostler or Roger Twose got out, Lara would have gone in and, with no play possible on the third day, would have had no chance of extending his run of consecutive hundreds, because reciprocal declarations were necessary in order to produce an outright result.

The captains, Andy Hayhurst and Tim Munton, argued their way through various mathematical equations, finally settling on Warwickshire chasing 321 in a minimum of 95 overs. Lara went in just before lunch and scored five out of 87 for one when the rains came.

Play restarted at 4 p.m., with the target now a wildly improbable 234 from 31 overs, and I started to write my match report, on the basis that rain had prevented Lara from trying for a fifth successive hundred. Warwickshire scorer Alec Davis sowed one seed of doubt as he entered his box, adjoining our press hutch. 'I've just asked Brian what to expect and he said, "Some crash, some bang and definitely plenty of wallop."'

Good quote I thought, but even if he got a hundred off his half of the strike, Warwickshire still had no chance of scoring at 15 runs every two overs, and play would be called off at 5.30 p.m., so I could compose for the morning readers with safety.

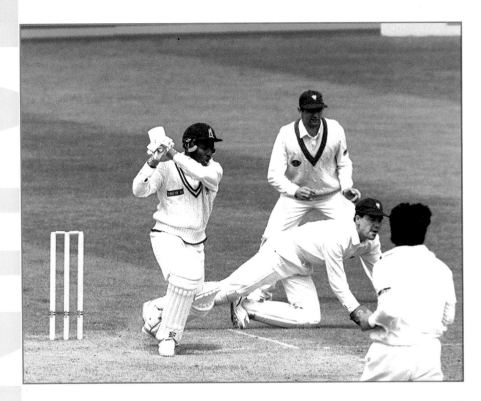

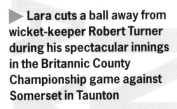

▶ **Lara cuts a ball away from wicket-keeper Robert Turner during his spectacular innings in the Britannic County Championship game against Somerset in Taunton**

That view was reinforced when Lara ran out Ostler in the 27th over for 51 out of 96 for two. It was a real pull-up of the gangplank, with common decency calling for Lara to go but, as I wrote, 'Instinct took over, and instinct was proved right.'

Paul Smith came and went for a breezy 38 off 31 balls but, when he was out, a score of 170 for three in 36 overs, with Lara then only on 37, meant that the game was destined for the dustbin of draws. How could a side score 151 from 21 overs on a pudding of an out-field, with large lateral boundaries more than offsetting the batting advantage of short straight boundaries at Taunton?

What followed was brutal and spectacular beyond belief. Lara's partner was Asif Din, no slouch at quick scoring himself, who stood as open-mouthed as the rest of us as Lara's natural scoring rate of a boundary an over was increased with a power of stroke that con-quered the sodden outfield. The milestones flashed by, over by over, and within half an hour, my carefully written report about a dull drawn match was wiped from my lap-top, and I just closed the lid to make notes of the mayhem I was watching.

Crash, bang, wallop he promised, and crash, bang, wallop he delivered. If we thought that his first 50 off 51 balls was something of a fireworks display, the pyrotechnics which followed lit up gloomy Taunton like the 20th Century Fox introduction clip to their films.

The 50 stand came off 32 balls and Din was seven. The target was now 111 off 17 overs, with Mushtaq Ahmed conceding ten or more runs in successive overs. Graham Rose had earlier let go two beamers at Lara and, perhaps coincidentally, perhaps not, he was hammered unmercifully for a final analysis of 18.4–1–117–0.

The longest boundary for Lara, batting at the new pavilion end, was the one at deep square leg, over which Lara casually flicked an enormous six off Rose to go from 93 to 99. We already knew that the fastest hundred was in his sights although, on 91 from 69 balls, he was odds against until he hit that wonderful six. A scampered two took him to 101 out of 251, with his second fifty having come off only 21 balls. Marvellous batting, which tore the Somerset attack to shreds.

His manipulation of the strike was brilliant. When the 100 stand came up off 61 balls, Din's share was 22 off the 21 balls he had been allowed and, by now, the game was more or less decided, with the target shrinking from 70 off 13 overs to 25 off six when Lara was finally bowled by Mushtaq for 136 out of 294 for four. He only hit 68 in boundaries, yet his running between the wickets was so electrifying, that his last 83 runs came from 43 balls. The partnership had added 126 in 13 overs, with Din scoring 27 of them.

Lara's aggregate from Antigua onwards was now 884 in five innings, with one not out, and he travelled to Lord's for the game against Middlesex needing one more hundred to join Bradman, Fry and Procter as the only men ever to score six successive hundreds.

▲ **Another cracking square cut at Taunton off Mushtaq Ahmed on 23 May, 1994. Lara hit 136 off 94 balls including the then fastest hundred of the season off 72 balls. The fielder is Ian Fletcher**

t was not to be, although he only missed by a whisker, scoring a glorious 140 in the second innings. Rain prevented any play on the first day at Lord's, but he walked in to bat at 11.30 a.m. on Friday morning to play his least convincing innings of the summer. He edged his first single and then survived two confident lbw appeals by Angus Fraser to Umpire David Constant.

He reached 26 from 49 balls before it happened. New boy Richard Johnson bowled one at his hip, and a thin leg-side edge was triumphantly snapped up by wicket-keeper Keith Brown, and Lara's 'nothing shot' – his own description – meant that he had to start all over again.

▲ **Middlesex v Warwickshire at Lord's**

He got a first-ball duck in the Sunday League game, but normal service was resumed next day when he scored his first 100 from 111 balls and then hit Emburey for a massive six, slightly off-side on to the guttering on the pavilion roof immediately above the home dressing-room. For height and distance, it matched the hit by Glamorgan's Mike Llewellyn, also off Emburey, in the 1977 Gillette Cup Final, although that was dragged over mid-on, with more leverage available.

Lara's 140 came out of 222 added while he batted, and he faced 147 balls from which he hit 94 in boundaries. The pattern of his individual scoring rate was becoming metronomic. Give or take a few, he was scoring at an unheard-of rate in first-class cricket of a run a ball. Roughly two-thirds of his runs came in boundaries, and his share of the runs scored while he was at the crease was about the same proportion.

Mike Gatting was particularly impressed with his watchfulness and how, 'He even adjusted late to the swinging ball. That calls for high-class technique, and he's got it. He makes life difficult for a fielding captain, because he is so murderous to anything not exactly in the right slot. Bowlers can get away with nothing.'

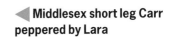

◀ Middlesex short leg Carr
peppered by Lara

◀ A tremendous powerful
square cut during his 140 in
the second innings of the
Middlesex match at Lord's

▶ Despondent after failing to score his sixth successive hundred

▼ Lara hits Emburey for a huge six on to the guttering of the south turret, immediately above the home dressing-room at Lord's. Bowler Emburey wonders 'What next?'

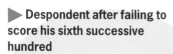

If a cricketer is lucky, destiny and history beckon once in a career. With good players, two or three times, but only the truly greats are favoured several times in one season. Lara had obliged with one world record in Antigua, and a record start with Warwickshire that had produced five hundreds in six innings, including a club record of four in his first four innings.

David Graveney telephoned me a couple of days before the start of Durham's four-day game at Edgbaston to discuss the likely pitch and, of course, Lara. I could offer him little comfort, although the first three days of the match gave little hint of the historic drama of the final day, aptly enough, D-Day, Monday, 6 June.

Individual records in cricket sometimes happen as a result of a freakish combination of match circumstances, and so it was at Edgbaston over the first weekend in June. The third day was wiped out by the weather, leaving Warwickshire 348 adrift of Durham's mammoth first-innings score of 558 for eight declared, with Lara hitting an unbeaten 111 off 143 balls.

His aggregate was now 1161 in 47 days, including seven hundreds in eight innings, the only batsman ever to do this – another world

▼ **End of a dream. Lara has just been caught behind for 26 off Richard Johnson of Middlesex. This dismissal followed five successive first-class hundreds**

record for him. With the third day washed out, the same sort of match situation obtained as at Taunton, with reciprocal declarations the obvious tactic.

I was at the Trent Bridge Test match, and telephoned the Edgbaston press box at about 11.15 a.m. to see what course the match was

taking. I was surprised to hear that the Durham captain, Phil Bainbridge, would not be drawn into any sort of declaration pact, because of injuries to two bowlers, and so the final day would be a contest for bonus points only.

The weather gods had been kind to Lara once again, because how many times, if ever, does a batsman receive an open cheque to bat all day? And even if he does, how many runs might he get in that day? Certainly not another 389 which Lara needed at the start of play to overtake Hanif Mohammad's 499.

Sheer curiosity brought three more telephone calls to Edgbaston before lunch, with the second one at 12.45 p.m. sounding the first alarm bell. In the hour between my second and third calls, Lara had sprinted from 144 to 254, and a personal lunch-time score of 285 convinced me that, although I was due to travel to London for the next day's televised Benson & Hedges Cup semi-final, I should divert from the M1 to the M42 and go to Edgbaston.

At 1.45 p.m. I drove out of Trent Bridge with John Thicknesse of the *Evening Standard*, and stayed in mobile telephonic contact with Edgbaston in case of the unlikely event of Lara's dismissal. I need not have worried. At 1.55 p.m. he registered the 107th score of 300 or more and, when I sprinted up the steps of the press box at 2.50 p.m., he was 370 and had already leap-frogged 96 of them, including Bradman's five triples, leaving the 452 temporarily dangling.

▲ **The County Championship match, Warwickshire v Durham, at Edgbaston, 6 June, 1994. Lara during his world-record innings of 501 not out. Keith Piper is the non-striker**

I caught up with the day's news, including the fact that Trevor Penney's share of a third-wicket partnership of 314 was 44. Also that while Penney scored 27 in the pre-lunch session, Lara hit 25 fours as he crashed his way from 111 to 285. Another seven runs, and he would have broken the record for the highest number of championship runs before lunch, which is 180 scored by K. S. Ranjitsinhji when he went from an overnight 54 to 234 in 1902 at Hastings against Surrey. That was a session of 150 minutes whereas Lara batted for 135.

Thicknesse and the local evening newspaper reporters willed Lara to beat Archie MacLaren's 424 by tea at 3.40 p.m., because of their deadlines, but they had to sit and suffer as he walked off with 418 in the book. That meant he had to score 82 more runs in no more than 90 minutes, because there was no chance of the game being extended past 5.30 p.m. unless a finish was possible. Even had the captains agreed to stay out there, Umpire Peter Wight insists that he would have drawn stumps, because the Test & County Cricket Board's regulations no longer carried any provision for an extension in a dead game.

Lara moves to 454, passing Don Bradman's 452, with a one-handed stroke only a brilliant improviser could execute

Bainbridge tried his hardest to deny Lara the strike, by spreading the field to give him a single when on strike, and bringing them in to save the single when partner Keith Piper was facing. In the next half an hour, a Pakistani (Aftab Baloch), an Australian (Bill Ponsford), an Indian (B. Nimbalkar) and then Bradman were crossed off Lara's shopping list. The press box was now a gibbering monkey-house with records being tossed to and fro like confetti.

Piper's maiden hundred went unnoticed as Lara's wedge of statistics became almost indigestible. The previous record number of runs in a day – 345 by Australian Charlie Macartney in 1921 against Nottinghamshire – was pocketed, and now only Hanif's 499 lay ahead. It became a race against time as the final half-hour was declared promptly at 5 p.m., with most people aware that curfew time might yet cruelly deny Lara the magic figure of 500. Most people – but not all, and certainly not as far as Lara was concerned.

In blissful ignorance, he ran singles to give Piper the strike, and was just happy to play his way towards the record. The 136th and final over of the match began at 5.28 p.m., bowled by John Morris, who was well aware that the final curtain was about to drop.

But on what? Lara was 497, two behind Hanif, and studiously blocked the first three balls. The fourth was an impudent, slow-medium bouncer which so took the history-maker by surprise that

**501**

▲ Graveney at gully, during the 501

it hit him on the helmet as he tried to paddle the ball for a single to long leg.

Had he succeeded, the outcome hardly bears thinking about. Lara would have been 498, at the non-striker's end with two balls of the match left. As it was, Piper thought it was about time he checked whether or not Lara knew the score. He did not but, once told that he had only two balls to move from 497, he promptly walloped the next ball through the covers and he was home.

For the second time in 49 days, almost to the minute, he had annexed a world individual record, and never before had one batsman held both records at Test and first-class level. What sort of monster was eating up the record-books so voraciously? Perhaps a clue to his remorseless approach is his choice of favourite film – *The Silence of the Lambs*.

His unbeaten 501 came thus, with the 10 fifties coming, respectively, off 60 balls, 58, 55, 27, 25, 33, 33, 39, 48 and 29. Note his progress from 150 to 250 – 52 balls – from 250 to 350 – 66 balls – and

finally, from 350 to 501, which came off 116 balls. He hit 62 fours – another individual record – and ten sixes, and shared in another partnership of over 300 with Piper, this one being worth 322.

His first reaction was that 'I am not yet a complete player.'

What his score did was to achieve near-perfect symmetry in runs from balls faced. He had now scored for Warwickshire 1176 runs from 1175 deliveries. That is nearly 1200 runs from all but 200 overs, and all done in the wash of Antigua and his 375.

◀ **Top of the world**

The innings took him to 2679 runs in 1994, over halfway towards a record he had not even heard about – Compton's calendar year aggregate of 4952 in 1947. Time to think of that later, because Edgbaston was a bedlam of microphones and reporters, all trying to talk to a man who was mentally and physically shot to pieces, and who still had to turn out next day in a knock-out semi-final.

Driving to London with Thicknesse, I listened to one interview in which Lara's media-battered state of mind was such that he even forgot how old he was. I heard him say that, 'As a 24-year-old I've got plenty of time to learn and get better.' He had celebrated his 25th birthday 35 days earlier.

▲ Warwickshire followers want to touch

▶ Partner Piper, with bowler Morris having just bowled the ball which took Lara from 497 to 501

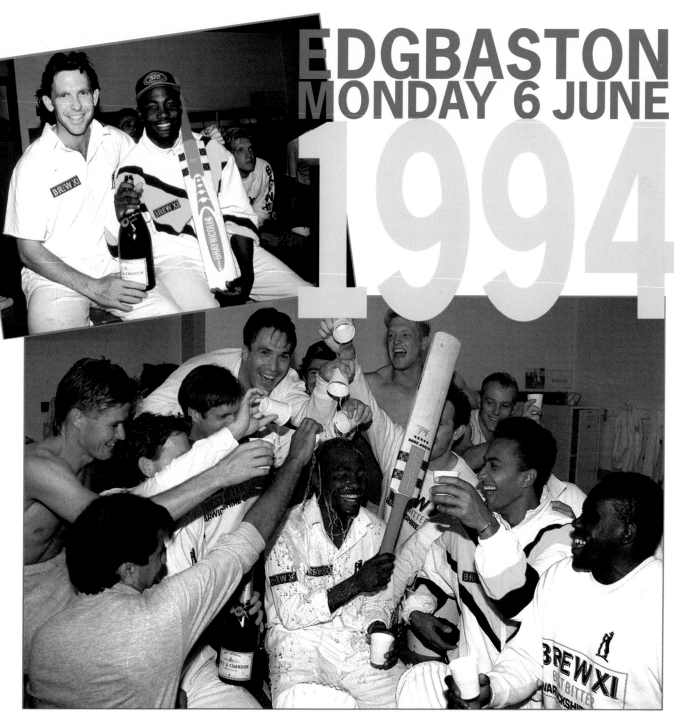

# EDGBASTON
## MONDAY 6 JUNE
# 1994

The next day's newspapers listed the records, but all missed one more. His 501 was the highest number of runs ever scored by one batsman in a first-class match. Self-evident? Not quite, because listed among those of four hundred or more, are three batsmen who have never scored a quadruple hundred. Graham Gooch scored 456 (333 + 123) at Lord's against India in 1990, Arthur Fagg scored 446 (244 + 202*) for Kent against Essex at Colchester in 1938, and Warwick Armstrong scored 402 (157* + 245) for Victoria against South Australia in Melbourne in 1920–21.

Lara celebrates his achievement with Captain Dermot Reeve ...

... and the delighted Warwickshire team

His innings had started tentatively. He was bowled by a no-ball and dropped by wicket-keeper Chris Scott, but an onslaught such as he launched is unlikely to be chanceless. On the final day, he was also dropped at long-off and a mis-hit to mid-wicket late in the innings fell short of the substitute fielder, who was his county colleague Michael Burns.

Dennis Amiss paid this tribute: 'I played in the matches when Glenn Turner got 311 and when Viv Richards scored 322, but this one goes way beyond that. We used to think when I played about how anyone could ever score 300 in a day. To get 390 like that was sheer magic. He has got that extra class for greatness.'

Warwickshire members present hit the jackpot. Some of them even ran into the ground when he was nearing 500. Mr Graham Walker said he heard what was happening on the radio and jumped into his car. 'I was stuck at the crossroads when he was on 490, and about a dozen of us ran across the car-park in time to see the last hit.'

Hanif Mohammad was contacted and said, 'I am happy to see him take my record. All records are made to be broken and it is good for cricket. I think one of his secrets is his height. He is very short and many other short players have scored lots of runs, like me, Sir Don Bradman and Sir Len Hutton.'

Lara's innings convinced me that comparisons with Bradman are now valid, because he is also a destroyer with a natural batting pace of a boundary an over. He has grace, balance, and a keenness of eye which enables him to pick up line and length quicker than most, and therefore he stands still longer, thus giving himself options denied to other batsmen. There is a mental side to batting as well. This is the part which remains a closed book to most, and only a partly open one to a few. Lara, like Bradman, is rewriting it, because of his discovery that four-day cricket provides a genius with the perfect showcase for enormous talent.

Almost unnoticed was the fact that, never mind the rare feat of scoring a hundred before lunch, on D-Day, 6 June, Lara scored 300 before tea.

An English season offers no let-up and, within 18 hours of walking off at Edgbaston, Lara had travelled the 120 miles to the Oval, knocked off a hundred-and-one interviews and was fielding against Surrey in the Benson & Hedges Cup semi-final.

The *Standard*'s John Thicknesse understandably thought that no human being could cope with such an important game so soon after a world record, and he seemed right when Lara left the field before the end of the home innings, complaining about dizziness and a headache.

Had it been possible, he would not have batted but, with his side in trouble, he came in at number six and hit a match-winning 70 which was an inspired innings. Curiously enough, it was his first real contribution in one-day cricket, but his presence in the Warwickshire dressing-room was inspirational enough to push the team into an unbeaten record in all competitions by the end of June.

He flew home to Trinidad the next day, but even that visit was cut short, because of his fulfilment of a commitment to play on John Paul Getty's ground the following Sunday. Warwickshire's sixth championship match was at home against Kent, and brought his first relative failure, with innings of 19 and 31.

◀ The next day in the Benson & Hedges semi-final at the Oval, Lara came in at number six due to fatigue, and hit a match-winning 70. Cameron Cuffy is the bowler

Had the bubble burst? Allan Lamb thought so, using that very phrase before the next match at Northampton, where much was made of the duel between Lara and Ambrose who, in four previous first-class matches, had never dismissed his Test colleague.

Lara's reply was magnificent. He scored 197 and, although he was worked over by Ambrose after tea, and was lucky to survive 24 blistering deliveries from which he managed two runs, his batting before tea was on a par with anything he had done for Warwickshire.

At tea, he was 160, 120 of which had come in boundaries, and he scored 140 out of 193 added in the afternoon session, with Penney again the willing sleeping partner. Lara's ability to improvise brought one of the most astounding strokes I have ever seen.

He danced down the pitch to drive slow left-arm bowler Nick Cook, but was nowhere near the pitch of the ball, thanks to the bowler seeing him coming and firing it in short.

With mother, Pearl

I'm not a right-hander, but this is what you do

He never forgets us

Unable to loft the ball in orthodox fashion, he took the bottom hand off the bat before impact and, with only the leading right hand on the top of the bat-handle, swatted a towering six over long-on. The bowler could scarcely believe his eyes, and small wonder.

One note of disquiet. In that match, and not for the first time, Lara was absent when Warwickshire fielded. Cricket can be that much easier if an individual is excused boots, but there must be a limit to what even a genius is allowed to do.

# SUMMING UP

So how best to sum up Lara the batsman and Lara the man? Bob Woolmer, one of the best analysts in the modern game says, 'He is as good as the best. And by that I include him with Sobers, both Viv and Barry Richards, and Graeme Pollock. Like them, he is almost impossible to bowl at, but the difference is he is younger than they were when they were at their best.

'I have never seen anyone hit the ball harder, but his greatest quality is his ability to hit the ball late and dead square. All the top players work across the line sometimes – Viv was a master of it – and Barry could play square both sides. It is very difficult to block scoring strokes in this area, because most field placings are at an angle.

'His placement comes purely from the top hand, which controls when he opens and closes the face of the bat, sometimes in mid-stroke when you think he is going to play straight. I think he is ready to hit every ball for four, until he has to block one. Most batsmen approach things the other way around – that is why he is the most exciting batsman in the world.

'A lot depends now on whether the grind of regular cricket gets to him, but he really is exceptionally strong mentally. It is frightening to think what he might do on better pitches in Test cricket because, when he decides that things are right for him, there is no limit to what he can do, as he has already shown against England in Antigua and Durham at Edgbaston. If anyone can break either of those two records, it is him.'

Nigel Briers agrees. 'He has good hands and a technique which, like that of David Gower, seems to work for him. He seems to handle everything so well, on and off the field. He has an amazing eye, and how he hits the ball so hard with a bat weighing 2 pounds seven ounces is beyond me. All the fierce hitters I have seen use heavy clubs, yet he whacks it around with a featherweight bat. Amazing. He has so many strokes you think he would give you a chance, but he doesn't.'

David Graveney has been in county cricket for 22 years, and makes this point about that huge Lara backlift. 'I have fielded in the gully a lot, and of course you have to watch the bat as the ball is bowled. I nearly went cross-eyed watching that flourish. It is the cricketing equivalent of golf's John Daley – past the horizontal on the backswing.'

That remark, coupled with the one from Woolmer about the huge rotation of the shoulders by Lara when he picks the bat up, seems to offer the best technical explanation of the basis of a method that, already at the age of 25, has set him apart from all other contemporary Test batsmen.

Regarding Lara the man, he has impressed his new Warwickshire colleagues with his innate modesty and dignity. That is not to say he is a recluse. Far from it. Nor is he a teetotaller, although he is careful about where and how much. He loves music, and also is not averse to going racing.

He has only three disciplinary indiscretions on an otherwise spotless record. The first two took place in the Caribbean, one concerning a dressing-room disagreement with his then captain, Gus Logie, for which he was fined TT$500. The other incident concerned a public altercation while out with his close friend, professional footballer Dwight Yorke, which ended with a trip to the police station and a dressing down from the sergeant on duty.

The third, in England, was the most serious. The three weeks following his world record 501 on 6 June, were fraught with physical and mental problems. He complained of fatigue and was frequently absent from the field when Warwickshire were fielding. For various reasons he spent an estimated 16 hours off the field and this, together with a series of missed practices and late reporting for playing duty on the mornings of matches, brought matters to a head.

On Sunday, 26 June at Northampton, half an hour before the start of the Sunday League match, he told the BBC's Jonathan Agnew that he was not going to play – not having spoken to either his captain, Dermot Reeve, or Director of Coaching, Bob Woolmer, beforehand.

He was ordered to play in the televised match, which was also the first ever all-ticket Sunday match at Northampton, made so mainly because of Lara, and was then spoken to about his attitude and an incident two days earlier on the field when he clashed with Reeve. The Club's Chief Executive, Dennis Amiss, met him on a one-to-one basis two days later and, with the player being reminded of his responsibilities to himself, his colleagues, the club and cricket, the matter was quickly resolved.

His behaviour was untypical of a man whose upbringing has instilled a sense of family values unusual in a modern sportsman, and the incidents sprang from understandable reaction to the mass-media attention to which he had been subjected.

Let the last word go to mother Pearl.

'To God be the glory. I am not happy for myself. I'm happy for Brian. He always wanted to be a cricketer, to do all the things he is doing, and I thank God he is doing it. I am not responsible for what he is doing. God is. I was used as the instrument to bring him into the world.'

# CAREER STATISTICS

## UP TO & INCLUDING 30 JULY 1994

### Compiled by Robert Brooke

**Abbreviations** (Excluding English county abbreviations)

| | | | | | | | |
|---|---|---|---|---|---|---|---|
| Adel | – Adelaide | Geo | – Georgetown, Guyana | NSW | – New South Wales | SR | – Sri Lanka |
| Aus | – Australia | Guy | – Guyana | Pak | – Pakistan | StGeo | – St Georges, Antigua |
| Barb | – Barbados | Har | – Harare | PaP | – Pointe-à-Pierre | StV | – St Vincent |
| Bass | – Basseterre | Jam | – Jamaica | QP | – Queen's Park, Port-of-Spain | TT | – Trinidad & Tobago |
| Cast | – Castries, St Lucia | Ken | – Kensington Oval, Barbados | RSC | – Red Stripe Cup | WAus | – Western Australia |
| Com | – Combined | LIs | – Leeward Islands | SA | – South Africa | WI | – West Indies |
| Edg'n | – Edgbaston | MCG | – Melbourne Cricket Ground | SabP | – Sabina Park, Jamaica | WIs | – Windward Islands |
| Ess | – Essequibo, Guyana | Mont | – Montserrat | Sarg | – Sargodha | Zim | – Zimbabwe |
| Frdly | – Friendly | Mor'a | – Moratuwa | Scarb | – Scarborough | † indicates that Lara was Captain | |

## Season 1987/88

### Playing for Trinidad & Tobago

| Dates | Venue | Opp | Comp | Inn | Pos | How dismissed | Runs | Cat | Result |
|---|---|---|---|---|---|---|---|---|---|
| 22.1.88 – 25.1.88 | PaP | LIs | RSC | 1 | 5 | c LL Harris b ET Willett | 14 | 1 | TT won by 2 wkts |
| | | | | 2 | 6 | st LL Harris b ET Willett | 22 | 1 | |
| 29.1.88 – 1.2.88 | QP | Barb | RSC | 1 | 4 | lbw J Garner | 92 | 3 | Match drawn |
| | | | | 2 | – | did not bat | – | 1 | |
| 5.2.88 – 8.2.88 | Ess | Guy | RSC | – | – | did not bat | – | – | Match drawn |

### Playing for West Indies Under-23s

| Dates | Venue | Opp | Comp | Inn | Pos | How dismissed | Runs | Cat | Result |
|---|---|---|---|---|---|---|---|---|---|
| †9.4.88 – 12.4.88 | Cast | Pak | Frdly | 1 | 3 | b Hafiz Shahid | 6 | 1 | Match drawn |
| | | | | 2 | 5 | lbw Zakirullah | 11 | 1 | |

### Averages

| | Mat | Inn | NO | Runs | HS | Av | 100s | 50s | Cat | Wkts | Runs |
|---|---|---|---|---|---|---|---|---|---|---|---|
| Season | 4 | 5 | 0 | 145 | 92 | 29.00 | – | 1 | 8 | – | 15 |
| Career | 4 | 5 | 0 | 145 | 92 | 29.00 | – | 1 | 8 | – | 15 |

## Season 1988/89

### Playing for Trinidad & Tobago

| Dates | Venue | Opp | Comp | Inn | Pos | How dismissed | Runs | Cat | Result |
|---|---|---|---|---|---|---|---|---|---|
| 20.1.89 – 23.1.89 | PaP | Guy | RSC | 1 | 4 | b JA Angus | 127 | 1 | TT lost by 5 wkts |
| | | | | 2 | 4 | lbw LA Joseph | 4 | – | |
| 27.1.89 – 30.1.89 | Ken | Barb | RSC | 1 | 4 | lbw MA Small | 77 | 3 | TT lost by 101 runs |
| | | | | 2 | 4 | b HAdaC Springer | 48 | – | |
| 10.2.89 – 12.2.89 | Nevis | LIs | RSC | 1 | 4 | c EAE Baptiste b KC Benjamin | 11 | – | TT lost by 186 runs |
| | | | | 2 | 3 | c LL Harris b EAE Baptiste | 9 | – | |
| 18.2.89 – 20.2.89 | PaP | Jam | RSC | 1 | 4 | c CA Davidson b RC Haynes | 36 | 1 | TT won by 10 wkts |
| | | | | 2 | – | did not bat | – | – | |
| 25.2.89 – 28.2.89 | StGeo | WIs | RSC | 1 | 4 | b TZ Kentish | 24 | 1 | Match drawn |
| | | | | 2 | – | did not bat | – | – | |

**Playing for President's XI**

| Dates | Venue | Opp | Comp | Inn | Pos | How dismissed | Runs | Cat | Result |
|---|---|---|---|---|---|---|---|---|---|
| 2.3.89 – 5.3.89 | Ken | India | Frdly | 1 | 5 | run out | 16 | 1 | Match drawn |
| | | | | 2 | 4 | lbw K Srikkanth | 33 | 1 | |

**Playing for West Indies Under 23s**

| Dates | Venue | Opp | Comp | Inn | Pos | How dismissed | Runs | Cat | Result |
|---|---|---|---|---|---|---|---|---|---|
| †14.3.89 – 17.3.89 | Bass | India | Frdly | 1 | 4 | c K Srikkanth b NS Hirwani | 182 | – | Match drawn |
| | | | | 2 | – | did not bat | – | – | |

**Playing for Board XI**

| Dates | Venue | Opp | Comp | Inn | Pos | How dismissed | Runs | Cat | Result |
|---|---|---|---|---|---|---|---|---|---|
| 1.4.89 – 4.4.89 | Arnos | India | Frdly | 1 | – | did not bat | – | – | Match drawn |
| | | | | 2 | – | did not bat | – | – | |

**Averages**

| | Mat | Inn | NO | Runs | HS | Av | 100s | 50s | Cat | Wkts | Runs |
|---|---|---|---|---|---|---|---|---|---|---|---|
| Season | 8 | 11 | 0 | 567 | 182 | 47.25 | 2 | 1 | 8 | – | – |
| Career | 12 | 16 | 0 | 712 | 182 | 44.50 | 2 | 2 | 16 | – | 15 |

## Season 1989/90

**Playing for West Indies 'B'**

| Dates | Venue | Opp | Comp | Inn | Pos | How dismissed | Runs | Cat | Result |
|---|---|---|---|---|---|---|---|---|---|
| †10.10.89 – 13.10.89 | Har | Zim XI | Frdly | 1 | 4 | c I Butchart b EA Brandes | 145 | – | Match drawn |
| | | | | 2 | – | did not bat | – | – | |
| †24.10.89 – 26.10.89 | Har | Zim XI | Frdly | 1 | 4 | c DL Houghton b K Duers | 35 | 1 | WI won by inns |
| | | | | 2 | – | did not bat | – | – | + 230 runs |
| †31.10.89 – 3.11.89 | Har | Zim XI | Frdly | 1 | 4 | b K Duers | 7 | 1 | WI won by inns |
| | | | | 2 | – | did not bat | – | 3 | + 56 runs |

**Averages**

| | Mat | Inn | NO | Runs | HS | Av | 100s | 50s | Cat | Wkts | Runs |
|---|---|---|---|---|---|---|---|---|---|---|---|
| Tour | 3 | 3 | 0 | 187 | 145 | 62.33 | 1 | – | 5 | – | – |
| Career | 15 | 19 | 0 | 899 | 182 | 47.31 | 3 | 2 | 21 | – | 15 |

**Playing for Trinidad & Tobago**

| Dates | Venue | Opp | Comp | Inn | Pos | How dismissed | Runs | Cat | Result |
|---|---|---|---|---|---|---|---|---|---|
| †5.1.90 – 8.1.90 | SabP | Jam | RSC | 1 | 4 | b RC Haynes | 33 | 1 | TT lost by 58 runs |
| | | | | 2 | 4 | c PJL Dujon b RC Haynes | 9 | 2 | |
| †12.1.90 – 15.1.90 | PaP | WIs | RSC | 1 | 3 | c DA Joseph b IBE Allen | 2 | 2 | TT lost by 4 wkts |
| | | | | 2 | 3 | lbw WW Davis | 14 | 1 | |
| †19.1.90 – 22.1.90 | QP | WIs | RSC | 1 | 4 | b HA Anthony | 27 | 2 | TT lost by 8 wkts |
| | | | | 2 | 4 | c LL Harris b EAE Baptiste | 15 | – | |
| †26.1.90 – 29.1.90 | PaP | Bar | RSC | 1 | 4 | b HAdaC Springer | 45 | – | TT lost by inns |
| | | | | 2 | 4 | c RL Hoyte b VdeC Walcott | 33 | – | + 87 runs |

**Playing for President's XI**

| Dates | Venue | Opp | Comp | Inn | Pos | How dismissed | Runs | Cat | Result |
|---|---|---|---|---|---|---|---|---|---|
| 17.3.90 – 20.3.90 | PaP | Eng XI | Frdly | 1 | 4 | b PAJ DeFreitas | 134 | – | WI lost by 113 runs |
| | | | | 2 | 4 | lbw PAJ DeFreitas | 1 | – | |

**Averages**

| | Mat | Inn | NO | Runs | HS | Av | 100s | 50s | Cat | Wkts | Runs |
|---|---|---|---|---|---|---|---|---|---|---|---|
| Season | 5 | 10 | 0 | 313 | 134 | 31.30 | 1 | – | 8 | – | 2 |
| Career | 20 | 29 | 0 | 1212 | 182 | 41.79 | 4 | 2 | 29 | – | 17 |

## Season 1990/91

### Playing for West Indies

| Dates | Venue | Opp | Comp | Inn | Pos | How dismissed | Runs | Cat | Result |
|---|---|---|---|---|---|---|---|---|---|
| 1.12.90 – 3.12.90 | Sarg | Com XI | Frdly | 1 | 4 | b Naeem Khan | 139 | – | Match drawn |
|  |  |  |  | 2 | 6 | not out | 24 | – |  |
| 6.12.90 – 11.12.90 | Lahore | Pak | Test | 1 | 4 | c A Malik b Abdul Qadir | 44 | – | Match drawn |
|  |  |  |  | 2 | 4 | c S Malik b Imran Khan | 5 | 1 |  |

**Averages**

| | Mat | Inn | NO | Runs | HS | Av | 100s | 50s | Cat | Wkts | Runs |
|---|---|---|---|---|---|---|---|---|---|---|---|
| Tour | 2 | 4 | 1 | 212 | 139 | 70.66 | 1 | – | 1 | – | – |
| Career | 22 | 33 | 1 | 1424 | 182 | 44.50 | 5 | 2 | 30 | – | 17 |

### Playing for Trinidad & Tobago

| Dates | Venue | Opp | Comp | Inn | Pos | How dismissed | Runs | Cat | Result |
|---|---|---|---|---|---|---|---|---|---|
| 4.1.91 – 7.1.91 | QP | LIs | RSC | 1 | 4 | run out | 7 | 1 | Match drawn |
|  |  |  |  | 2 | 4 | c EAE Baptiste b WK Benjamin | 71 | – |  |
| 11.1.91 – 14.1.91 | SabP | Jam | RSC | 1 | 4 | not out | 122 | – | Match drawn |
|  |  |  |  | 2 | 4 | c sub b CA Walsh | 87 | 1 |  |
| 18.1.91 – 21.1.91 | PaP | WIs | RSC | 1 | 4 | c and b TZ Kentish | 69 | – | TT won by 141 runs |
|  |  |  |  | 2 | 4 | run out | 96 | – |  |
| 25.1.91 – 28.1.91 | Ken | Barb | RSC | 1 | 4 | c CO Browne b AC Cummins | 67 | 4 | TT lost by 9 wkts |
|  |  |  |  | 2 | 4 | c CA Best b SM Skeete | 24 | – |  |
| 1.2.91 – 4.2.91 | PaP | Guy | RSC | 1 | 4 | c S Mohammed b CG Butts | 23 | – | Match drawn |
|  |  |  |  | 2 | 4 | b LA Joseph | 61 | – |  |
| 15.3.91 –17.3.91 | PaP | Aus | Frdly | 1 | 4 | c MRJ Veletta b BA Reid | 33 | – | Match drawn |
|  |  |  |  | 2 | – | did not bat | – | – |  |

### Playing for West Indies Under-23s

| Dates | Venue | Opp | Comp | Inn | Pos | How dismissed | Runs | Cat | Result |
|---|---|---|---|---|---|---|---|---|---|
| 30.3.91 – 2.4.91 | Arnos | Aus | Frdly | 1 | 4 | lbw TM Alderman | 22 | 3 | Match drawn |
|  |  |  |  | 2 | 4 | st MRJ Veletta b PL Taylor | 4 | – |  |

### Playing for West Indies Board XI

| Dates | Venue | Opp | Comp | Inn | Pos | How dismissed | Runs | Cat | Result |
|---|---|---|---|---|---|---|---|---|---|
| 13.4.91 – 17.4.91 | Ken | Aus | Frdly | 1 | 4 | c GR Marsh b SR Waugh | 56 | – | Match drawn |
|  |  |  |  | 2 | 4 | b TM Alderman | 36 | – |  |

**Averages**

| | Mat | Inn | NO | Runs | HS | Av | 100s | 50s | Cat | Wkts | Runs |
|---|---|---|---|---|---|---|---|---|---|---|---|
| Season | 8 | 15 | 1 | 778 | 122* | 55.57 | 1 | 7 | 9 | – | – |
| Career | 30 | 48 | 2 | 2202 | 182 | 47.87 | 6 | 9 | 39 | – | 17 |

## Season 1991

### Playing for West Indies

| Dates | Venue | Opp | Comp | Inn | Pos | How dismissed | Runs | Cat | Result |
|---|---|---|---|---|---|---|---|---|---|
| 15.5.91 – 17.5.91 | Worc | Worcs | Frdly | 1 | 4 | b PJ Newport | 26 | 1 | Match drawn |
|  |  |  |  | 2 | – | did not bat | – | – |  |
| 29.5.91 – 31.5.91 | Taunton | Som | Frdly | 1 | 4 | c and b HRJ Trump | 93 | 1 | Match drawn |
|  |  |  |  | 2 | 4 | c SJ Cook b DA Graveney | 50 | – |  |
| 1.6.91 – 3.6.91 | Leic | Leics | Frdly | 1 | 4 | c PA Nixon b JN Maguire | 3 | 1 | WI won by 6 wkts |
|  |  |  |  | 2 | 4 | c MI Gidley b JN Maguire | 26 | – |  |
| 12.6.91 – 14.6.91 | Derby | Derbys | Frdly | 1 | 4 | lbw SJ Base | 1 | – | Match drawn |
|  |  |  |  | 2 | 3 | lbw DG Cork | 20 | – |  |
| 15.6.91 – 17.6.91 | Noton | Nthants | Frdly | 1 | 3 | c NGB Cook b EAE Baptiste | 4 | – | Match drawn |
|  |  |  |  | 2 | – | did not bat | – | – |  |

## Season 1991 continued

| Dates | Venue | Opp | Comp | Inn | Pos | How dismissed | Runs | Cat | Result |
|---|---|---|---|---|---|---|---|---|---|
| 29.6.91 – 1.7.91 | Soton | Hants | Frdly | 1 | 4 | b SD Udal | 75 | – | Match drawn |
| | | | | 2 | – | did not bat | – | – | |
| 16.7.91 – 18.7.91 | Swansea | Glam | Frdly | 1 | 6 | c MP Maynard b M Frost | 6 | 1 | Match drawn |
| | | | | 2 | – | did not bat | – | – | |
| 20.7.91 – 22.7.91 | Cant | Kent | Frdly | 1 | 3 | lbw RM Ellison | 19 | 3 | WI won by 4 runs |
| | | | | 2 | 3 | b RP Davis | 18 | 2 | |

### Playing for West Indian XI

| Dates | Venue | Opp | Comp | Inn | Pos | How dismissed | Runs | Cat | Result |
|---|---|---|---|---|---|---|---|---|---|
| 28.8.91 – 30.8.91 | Scarb | Wor XI | Frdly | 1 | 4 | lbw DK Morrison | 2 | – | Match drawn |
| | | | | 2 | 6 | st PR Sleep b Maninder Singh | 1 | – | |

### Averages

| | Mat | Inn | NO | Runs | HS | Av | 100s | 50s | Cat | Wkts | Runs |
|---|---|---|---|---|---|---|---|---|---|---|---|
| Season | 9 | 14 | – | 344 | 93 | 24.57 | – | 3 | 9 | – | 59 |
| Career | 39 | 62 | 2 | 2546 | 182 | 42.43 | 6 | 12 | 48 | – | 76 |

## Season 1991/92

### Playing for West Indies

| Dates | Venue | Opp | Comp | Inn | Pos | How dismissed | Runs | Cat | Result |
|---|---|---|---|---|---|---|---|---|---|
| 20.12.91 – 23.12.91 | Hobart | Aus XI | Frdly | 1 | 3 | c WN Phillips b SK Warne | 83 | – | Aus XI won by inns |
| | | | | 2 | 3 | b CD Matthews | 10 | – | + 93 runs |

### Playing for Trinidad & Tobago

| Dates | Venue | Opp | Comp | Inn | Pos | How dismissed | Runs | Cat | Result |
|---|---|---|---|---|---|---|---|---|---|
| 24.1.92 – 27.1.92 | QP | Barb | RSC | 1 | 4 | c and b OD Gibson | 135 | – | Match drawn |
| | | | | 2 | 4 | c and b VD Walcott | 37 | – | |
| 31.1.92 – 3.2.92 | PaP | Guy | RSC | 1 | 4 | c SN Mohammed b RA Harper | 17 | – | Match drawn |
| | | | | 2 | – | did not bat | – | – | |
| 8.2.92 – 11.2.92 | QP | Jam | RSC | 1 | 4 | b CA Walsh | 12 | – | Match drawn |
| | | | | 2 | – | did not bat | – | 1 | |

### Playing for West Indies

| Dates | Venue | Opp | Comp | Inn | Pos | How dismissed | Runs | Cat | Result |
|---|---|---|---|---|---|---|---|---|---|
| 18.4.92 – 23.4.92 | Ken | SA | Test | 1 | 3 | c DJ Richardson b T Bosch | 17 | 3 | WI won by 52 runs |
| | | | | 2 | 3 | c DJ Richardson b AA Donald | 64 | 2 | |

### Averages

| | Mat | Inn | NO | Runs | HS | Av | 100s | 50s | Cat | Wkts | Runs |
|---|---|---|---|---|---|---|---|---|---|---|---|
| Season | 5 | 8 | – | 375 | 135 | 46.87 | 1 | 2 | 6 | – | 1 |
| Career | 44 | 70 | 2 | 2921 | 182 | 42.95 | 7 | 14 | 54 | – | 77 |

## Season 1992/93

### Playing for West Indies

| Dates | Venue | Opp | Comp | Inn | Pos | How dismissed | Runs | Cat | Result |
|---|---|---|---|---|---|---|---|---|---|
| 6.11.92 – 9.11.92 | Perth | W Aus | Frdly | 1 | 3 | c TM Moody b J Angel | 55 | 1 | WI won by |
| | | | | 2 | 3 | c JL Langer b J Angel | 46 | 1 | 236 runs |
| 20.11.92 – 23.11.92 | Sydney | NSW | Frdly | 1 | 2 | c PA Emery b WJ Holdsworth | 16 | 1 | Match drawn |
| | | | | 2 | 2 | c PA Emery b WJ Holdsworth | 3 | – | |
| 27.11.92 – 1.12.92 | Brisbane | Aus | Test | 1 | 4 | st IA Healy b GRJ Matthews | 58 | 2 | Match drawn |
| | | | | 2 | 4 | c MA Taylor b CJ McDermott | 0 | – | |
| 26.12.92 – 30.12.92 | MCG | Aus | Test | 1 | 4 | lbw MR Whitney | 52 | 2 | Aus won by |
| | | | | 2 | 4 | c DC Boon b MR Whitney | 4 | – | 139 runs |
| 2.1.93 – 6.1.93 | Sydney | Aus | Test | 1 | 4 | run out | 277 | – | Match drawn |
| | | | | 2 | – | did not bat | – | – | |

## Season 1992/93 continued

| Dates | Venue | Opp | Comp | Inn | Pos | How dismissed | Runs | Cat | Result |
|---|---|---|---|---|---|---|---|---|---|
| 23.1.93 – 26.1.93 | Adelaide | Aus | Test | 1 | 4 | c IA Healy b CJ McDermott | 52 | – | WI won by 1 wkt |
| | | | | 2 | 4 | c SR Waugh b MG Hughes | 7 | – | |
| 30.1.93 – 1.2.93 | Perth | Aus | Test | 1 | 4 | c SK Warne b CJ McDermott | 16 | 1 | WI won by inns |
| | | | | 2 | – | did not bat | – | 1 | + 25 runs |

### Averages

| | Mat | Inn | NO | Runs | HS | Av | 100s | 50s | Cat | Wkts | Runs |
|---|---|---|---|---|---|---|---|---|---|---|---|
| Tour | 7 | 12 | – | 586 | 277 | 48.83 | 1 | 4 | 9 | – | 4 |
| Career | 51 | 82 | 2 | 3507 | 277 | 48.83 | 8 | 18 | 63 | – | 81 |

### Playing for West Indies

| Dates | Venue | Opp | Comp | Inn | Pos | How dismissed | Runs | Cat | Result |
|---|---|---|---|---|---|---|---|---|---|
| 16.4.93 – 18.4.93 | QP | Pak | Test | 1 | 4 | c A Sohail b Waqar Younis | 6 | 2 | WI won by 204 runs |
| | | | | 2 | 4 | b Asif Mujtaba | 96 | – | |
| 23.4.93 – 27.4.93 | Ken | Pak | Test | 1 | 4 | c Moin Khan b A–ur–Rehman | 51 | – | WI won by 10 wkts |
| | | | | 2 | – | did not bat | – | 1 | |
| 1.5.93 – 6.5.93 | St Johns | Pak | Test | 1 | 4 | st R Latif b Nadeem Khan | 44 | – | Match drawn |
| | | | | 2 | 4 | lbw Waqar Younis | 19 | – | |

### Averages

| | Mat | Inn | NO | Runs | HS | Av | 100s | 50s | Cat | Wkts | Runs |
|---|---|---|---|---|---|---|---|---|---|---|---|
| Series | 3 | 5 | – | 216 | 96 | 43.20 | – | 2 | 3 | – | – |
| Career | 54 | 87 | 2 | 3723 | 277 | 43.80 | 8 | 20 | 66 | – | 81 |

# Season 1993/94

### Playing for West Indies

| Dates | Venue | Opp | Comp | Inn | Pos | How dismissed | Runs | Cat | Result |
|---|---|---|---|---|---|---|---|---|---|
| 8.12.93 – 13.12.93 | Mor'a | SR | Test | 1 | 4 | c P Dassanayake b M Muralitharan | 18 | 3 | Match drawn |
| | | | | 2 | – | did not bat | – | – | |

### Averages

| | Mat | Inn | NO | Runs | HS | Av | 100s | 50s | Cat | Wkts | Runs |
|---|---|---|---|---|---|---|---|---|---|---|---|
| Tour | 1 | 1 | – | 18 | 18 | 18.00 | – | – | 3 | – | – |
| Career | 55 | 88 | 2 | 3741 | 277 | 43.50 | 8 | 20 | 69 | – | 81 |

### Playing for Trinidad & Tobago

| Dates | Venue | Opp | Comp | Inn | Pos | How dismissed | Runs | Cat | Result |
|---|---|---|---|---|---|---|---|---|---|
| †7.1.94 – 10.1.94 | Castries | WIs | RSC | 1 | 4 | c J Eugene b CE Cuffy | 5 | 3 | TT won by 1 wkt |
| | | | | 2 | 4 | c JR Murray b CE Cuffy | 28 | 1 | |
| †14.1.94 – 16.1.94 | Mont | LIs | RSC | 1 | 4 | c and b KCG Benjamin | 2 | 1 | LIs won by inns |
| | | | | 2 | 4 | b WD Phillip | 84 | – | + 110 runs |
| †21.1.94 – 24.1.94 | QP | Jam | RSC | 1 | 4 | c RW Staple b RC Haynes | 180 | 2 | TT won by 3 wkts |
| | | | | 2 | 4 | lbw NO Perry | 23 | 4 | |
| †28.1.94 – 31.4.94 | PaP | Guy | RSC | 1 | 4 | c KA Wong b CL Hooper | 18 | 2 | TT won by 78 runs |
| | | | | 2 | 3 | run out | 169 | 1 | |
| †4.2.94 – 7.2.94 | QP | Barb | RSC | 1 | 4 | c SL Campbell b AC Cummins | 206 | – | Match drawn |
| | | | | 2 | – | did not bat | – | – | |

### Playing for West Indies

| Dates | Venue | Opp | Comp | Inn | Pos | How dismissed | Runs | Cat | Result |
|---|---|---|---|---|---|---|---|---|---|
| 19.2.94 – 24.2.94 | SabP | Eng | Test | 1 | 4 | b GA Hick | 83 | – | WI won by 8 wkts |
| | | | | 2 | 3 | b AR Caddick | 28 | – | |
| 17.3.94 – 22.3.94 | GeoT | Eng | Test | 1 | 3 | c MA Atherton c CC Lewis | 167 | 1 | WI won by inns |
| | | | | 2 | – | did not bat | – | – | + 44 runs |
| 25.3.94 – 30.3.94 | QP | Eng | Test | 1 | 3 | lbw CC Lewis | 43 | 3 | WI won by 147 runs |
| | | | | 2 | 3 | c IDK Salisbury b AR Caddick | 12 | 2 | |
| 8.4.94 – 13.4.94 | Ken | Eng | Test | 1 | 3 | c sub b CC Lewis | 26 | 1 | Eng won by 208 runs |
| | | | | 2 | 3 | c PCR Tufnell b AR Caddick | 64 | 2 | |

| Dates | Venue | Opp | Comp | Inn | Pos | How dismissed | Runs | Cat | Result |
|---|---|---|---|---|---|---|---|---|---|
| 16.4.94 – 21.4.94 | St Johns | Eng | Test | 1 | 3 | c RC Russell b AR Caddick | 375 | – | Match drawn |
|  |  |  |  | 2 | – | did not bat | – | – |  |

**Averages**

|  | Mat | Inn | NO | Runs | HS | Av | 100s | 50s | Cat | Wkts | Runs |
|---|---|---|---|---|---|---|---|---|---|---|---|
| Season | 10 | 17 | – | 1513 | 375 | 89.00 | 5 | 3 | 23 | 1 | 22 |
| Career | 65 | 105 | 2 | 5254 | 375 | 51.00 | 13 | 23 | 92 | 1 | 103 |

## Season 1994

**Playing for Warwickshire**

| Dates | Venue | Opp | Comp | Inn | Pos | How dismissed | Runs | Cat | Result |
|---|---|---|---|---|---|---|---|---|---|
| 28.4.94 – 1.5.94 | Edg'n | Glam | CC | 1 | 3 | c MP Maynard b RD Croft | 147 | – | Warks won by inns |
|  |  |  |  | 2 | – | did not bat | – | – | + 103 runs |
| 5.5.94 – 9.5.94 | Edg'n | Leics | CC | 1 | 3 | c and b ARK Pierson | 106 | – | Match drawn |
|  |  |  |  | 2 | 3 | not out | 120 | – |  |
| 19.5.94 – 23.5.94 | Taunton | Som | CC | 1 | – | Warks forfeited first inns | – | – | Warks won by 6 wkts |
|  |  |  |  | 2 | 3 | b Mushtaq Ahmed | 136 | 2 |  |
| 27.5.94 – 30.5.94 | Lord's | Middx | CC | 1 | 3 | c KR Brown b RL Johnson | 26 | 2 | Match drawn |
|  |  |  |  | 2 | 3 | c and b JE Emburey | 140 | – |  |
| 2.6.94 – 6.6.94 | Edg'n | Dur | CC | 1 | 3 | not out | 501 | 1 | Match drawn |
|  |  |  |  | 2 | – | no second inns | – | – |  |
| 16.6.94 – 20.6.94 | Edg'n | Kent | CC | 1 | 3 | c MV Fleming b MM Patel | 19 | – | Warks won by 76 runs |
|  |  |  |  | 2 | 3 | b CL Hooper | 31 | – |  |
| 23.6.94 – 27.6.94 | Noton | Nthants | CC | 1 | 3 | c MB Loye b JP Taylor | 197 | – | Warks won by 4 wkts |
|  |  |  |  | 2 | 7 | c AJ Lamb b NGB Cook | 2 | – |  |
| 14.7.94–18.7.94 | Guildford | Surrey | CC | 1 | 3 | c GP Thorpe b C Cuffy | 2 | – | Warks won by |
|  |  |  |  | 2 | 3 | c and b ACS Pigott | 44 | – | 256 runs |
| 21.7.94–23.7.94 | Edg'n | Essex | CC | 1 | 3 | c NS Knight b RC Irani | 70 | – | Warks won by |
|  |  |  |  | 2 | 3 | lbw RC Irani | 9 | 1 | 203 runs |
| 28.7.94–1.8.94 | Chesterfield | Derbys | CC | 1 | 3 | c KJ Barnett b DG Cork | 142 | – | Warks won by |
|  |  |  |  | 2 | 3 | lbw SJ Base | 51 | – | 139 runs |

**Averages**

|  | Mat | Inn | NO | Runs | HS | Av | 100s | 50s | Cat | Wkts | Runs |
|---|---|---|---|---|---|---|---|---|---|---|---|
| Season | 10 | 17 | 2 | 1743 | 501* | 116.20 | 8 | 2 | 6 | – | 180 |
| Career | 75 | 122 | 4 | 6997 | 501* | 59.29 | 21 | 25 | 98 | 1 | 283 |

## 501 Not out – the details

**Friday 3 June 1994**

| | |
|---|---|
| In | 3.28pm with Warwicks 8–1 |
| Tea | 18* in score of 66–1 (wose 30*) |
|  | 50 in 97 mins & 80 balls (6x4) |
|  | 100 in 144 mins & 138 balls (14x4) |
| Close | 111* out of total of 210–2 in 43 overs |

**Saturday 4 June 1994**

no play due to rain

**Monday 6 June 1994**

| | |
|---|---|
|  | 150 in 201 mins & 193 balls (22x4) |
|  | 200 in 224 mins & 220 balls (30x4 2x6) |
|  | 250 in 246 mins & 245 balls (37x4 5x6) |
| Lunch | 285* out of total of 423–2 in 78 overs |
|  | 300 in 280 mins & 278 balls (44x4 7x6) |
|  | 350 in 319 mins & 311 balls (49x4 8x6) |
|  | 400 in 367 mins & 350 balls (53x4 8x6) |
| Tea | 418* out of total of 636–4 in 109 overs |
|  | 450 in 430 mins & 398 balls (55x4 9x6) |
|  | 501 in 474 mins & 427 balls (62x4 10x6) |

# Milestones passed during innings

100* Completes 7th century in 8 consecutive innings – unique achievement in first-class cricket. In previous innings Brian Lara had achieved 6 centuries in 7 innings, to equal Ernest Tyldesley (1926), V Merchant (1940/41–1941/42), WR Hammond (1945–46), PN Kirsten (1976/77). Only 4th batsman to score 7 centuries in 9 innings, with CB Fry (1901), E Tyldesley (1926), DG Bradman (4 times, in 1931/32, 1937/38–1938, 1938–1938/39, 1947/48–48).
  6th century in 7 Championship innings – unique feat.
148* Achieves his highest score for Warwickshire.
248* Highest score in any first-class match against Durham – beating 247 by C Lewis for Notts in 1993.
278* Records highest score at Edgbaston by any batsman, any side, and highest score for Warwickshire by a left-hander. Previous holder of both records – RG Twose, 277* v Glamorgan in 1994.
285* Lunch. 174 runs before lunch, a new Warwickshire record, beating FR Santall (173 v Northants, Northampton 1933).
297* 3rd wicket stand of 314 in 55 overs with TL Penney – best for any wicket against Durham in first-class cricket.
301* First triple century at Edgbaston for any team.
306* New Warwickshire record for individual score – beating 305* by FR Foster v Worcestershire at Dudley in 1914.
323* Highest score in England by a West Indian – beating 322 by IVA Richards, Somerset against Warwickshire, Taunton 1985.
325* Reaches 1000 runs for season in 7th innings – equalling record of DG Bradman (Australians) in 1938.
  1000th run on 7th June, a new Warwickshire record, beating WJ Stewart (12th June) in 1962.
367* Highest score by left-hander in England, beating 366 by NH Fairbrother, Lancashire v Surrey, The Oval 1990.
376* Highest score by a West Indian – beating his own 375 for West Indies against England at St John's 1993/94.
386* Highest ever score by a left-hander – beating B Sutcliffe's 385, Otago v Canterbury, Christchurch 1952/53.
406* Highest score in England this century, beating GA Hicks 405*, Worcestershire v Somerset, Taunton 1988.
413* 19th player to score 300 runs in a day.
418* Tea. 133 runs between lunch and tea; first Warwicks player to score 100 or more runs in first two sessions of days play.
423* 274 runs (55 fours, 9 sixes) from strokes worth four or more beats record of 272 (68 fours) – PA Perrin (343*) Essex v Derbyshire, Chesterfield 1904.
425* Beats AC MacLaren's 424, Lancashire v Somerset, Taunton 1895 for highest score in English first-class cricket.
454* Passes DG Bradman, 452*, New South Wales v Queensland, Sydney 1929/30, for 2nd highest first-score.
458* Most runs by batsman in a day, overtaking CG Macartney's 345, Australians v Nottinghamshire, Trent Bridge 1921.
475* 69th hit worth 4 runs or more (60 fours, 9 sixes) beat record of 68 (all fours) by PA Perrin (343*) Essex v Derbys, Chesterfield 1904.
501* Boundary off JE Morris sees new first-class individual record score, beating 499 by Hanif Mohammad, Karachi v Bahawalpur, Karachi 1958/59.

# Other interesting happenings during innings

## Partnerships

Lara (0–46*) & RG Twose (0*–51) added 115 for 2nd wicket.
Lara (46*–297*) & TL Penney (0–44) added 314 for 3rd wicket in 185 minutes and 55.1 overs.
Lara (336*–501*) & KJ Piper (0–116*) added unbroken 322 for 5th wicket in 162 minutes and 45.1 overs. Both 3rd and 5th wicket stands broke the previous first-class partnership record against Durham for any wicket.

The stand of 322 beat the previous Warwickshire 5th wicket record of 268, by William and Walter Quaife against Essex at Leyton in 1900. It was the highest two man 5th wicket stand in county cricket since D Brookes and DW Barrick added 347 for Northants against Essex at Northampton in 1952.

For the first time in English first-class cricket, and the second in all, two stands in excess of 300 occurred in the same innings; it follows that Lara is the first batsman to be involved in two such stands in the same innings in English cricket.

## Miscellaneous

802 runs were scored while Lara was at the wicket, a new Warwickshire record beating the 657 scored during RG Twose's 277* against Glamorgan at Edgbaston earlier in 1994. Lara's total is the second best ever in England, beaten only by the 811 runs which R Abel batted out during his 357* for Surrey against Somerset at The Oval in 1899.

In addition to Lara's total of 501 runs being the most in any first-class innings, it was also the most in a match. The previous record was the 499 Hanif Mohammad scored in his only innings for Karachi against Bahawalpur in 1958/59.

## Runs in sequences of innings

Lara scored 641 in 2 innings, beating the previous record of WH Ponsford 639 (437 & 202) for Victoria 1927/28.

From his 375 for West Indies at St John's to his 501* Lara scored 1551 runs in 8 innings, beating the previous record of 1400 by WH Ponsford (Victoria) over Australian seasons 1926/27 and 1927/28. Lara's 1615 runs in 9 innings and 1641 in 10, 1798 in 11 and 1862 in 12, also beat records previously held by Ponsford, 1412 in 9 and 1582 in 10, 1733 in 11, and DG Bradman, 1837 in 12. Ponsford holds the records for most runs in consecutive innings from 13 to 16, while from 17 onwards Bradman takes over.

Finally, in the first innings of the last match covered in this survey Lara, when scoring 197, completed 8 centuries in 11 consecutive innings, equalling the feat of DG Bradman in 1938 and 1938/39.

# Statistical miscellany

**Major stands involving Brian Lara**

**1988/89**
120–3  with KA Williams, TT v Guyana, PaP

**1989/90**
205–4  with DA Joseph, WI 'B' v Zimb, Harare
100–3  with CB Lambert, WI 'B' v Zimb, Harare
127–4  with AL Logie, Pres XI v Eng XI, PaP

**1990/91**
170–3  with CG Greenidge, WI XI v Comb XI,Sargodha
100–4  with AL Logie, TT v Jam, Sabina P
117–6  with D Williams, TT v Windwards, PaP
139–3  with PV Simmons, TT v Guyana, PaP

**1991**
110–4  with CL Hooper, WI XI v Hants, Soton

**1992/93**
112–4  with KLT Arthurton, WI v Aust, Brisbane
106–4  with KLT Arthurton, WI v Aust, MCG
293–3  with RB Richardson, WI v Aust, Sydney
114–4  with KLT Arthurton, WI v Aust, Sydney
169–3  with DL Haynes, WI v Pak, QP
103–3  with DL Haynes, WI v Pak, Ken Oval

**1993/94**
105–8  with R Dhanraj, TT v Jamaica, QP
178–2  with S Ragoonath, TT v Guyana, PaP
108–3  with PV Simmons, TT v Barbados, QP
216–4  with K Mason, TT v Barbados, QP
167–4  with KLT Arthurton, WI v Eng,SabP
114–2  with DL Haynes, WI v Eng, Bourda
112–4  with JC Adams, WI v Eng, Bourda
179–3  with JC Adams, WI v Eng, St John's
183–4  with KLT Arthurton, WI v Eng, St John's
219–4  with S Chanderpaul, WI v Eng, St John's

**1994**
215–2  with RG Twose, Warks v Glamorgan, Edgbaston
102–2  with RG Twose, Warks v Leics, Edgbaston
126–4  with Asif Din, Warks v Somerset, Taunton
115–4  with PA Smith, Warks v Middlesex, Lord's
115–2  With RG Twose, Warks v Durham, Edgbaston
314–3  with TL Penney, Warks v Durham, Edgbaston
322–5* with KJ Piper, Warks v Durham, Edgbaston
168–4  with TL Penney, Warks v Northants, Northampton
160–4  with TL Penney, Warks v Derbys, Chesterfield

Lara scored his first first-class century, for Trinidad & Tobago v Guyana at Pointe–à–Pierre, in January 1989 aged 19 years, 264 days. His 127 occupied 310 minutes, he hit 15 fours, and faced 277 balls.

Lara's second first-class century was 182 for the West Indies Under–23 team, which he captained, aged still under 20, against the Indian tourists at Basseterre in March 1989. Lara's 182 occupied 345 minutes and included 21 fours and a six.

In his final innings of the 1991 Red Stripe Cup Competition, for Trinidad & Tobago against Guyana at Pointe–à–Pierre, Lara reached a total for the season of 627 runs (av.69.66), thus beating the previous record of 572 held by Ralston Otto (Leewards) since 1983/84. A few days later DL Haynes (Barbados) overtook Lara, to finish with 654 runs. In the 1994 competition Lara regained the record, scoring 715 runs, average 79.44.

Against Australia at Sydney, in 1992/93, Lara scored his maiden Test century, 277 in 474 minutes from 372 balls, with 38 fours, in his 5th Test. He reached his century in 125 balls. His 277 was the highest score in Tests between West Indies & Australia; it was the third highest Test score against Australia (after L Hutton, 364 and RE Foster 287, both for England), and the fourth highest on Australian soil (after RM Cowper, 307 & DG Bradman 299*, both Australia, and RE Foster, 287, England).

When Brian Lara scored 375 against England at St John's Antigua in the final Test of the 1993/94 series with England he set a new record individual score for Test cricket, beating the 365* by GS Sobers for West Indies against Pakistan at Sabina Park, Kingston in 1957/58.

## All Test scores in excess of 300

375  BC Lara, WI v Eng, St John's 1993/94
365* GS Sobers, WI v Pak, Sabina P 1957/58
364  L Hutton, Eng v Aust, The Oval 1938
337  Hanif Mohammad, Pak v WI, Ken Oval 1957/58
336* WR Hammond, Eng v NZ, Auckland 1932/33
334  DG Bradman, Aust v Eng, Leeds 1930
333  GA Gooch, Eng v Ind, Lord's 1990

325  A Sandham, Eng v WI, Sabina P 1929/30
311  RB Simpson, Aust v Eng, Old Trafford 1964
310* JH Edrich, Eng v NZ, Leeds 1965
307  RM Cowper, Aust v Eng, MCG 1965/66
304  DG Bradman, Aust v Eng, Leeds 1934
302  LG Rowe, WI v Eng, Ken Oval 1973/74

Lara broke the all-time individual scoring record for first-class cricket when scoring 501 not out for Warwickshire against Durham at Edgbaston in June 1994. He beat the previous record of 499 by Hanif Mohammad, for Karachi v Bahawalpur at Karachi in 1958/59.

# Brian Lara's career in limited-overs cricket

## Playing for West Indies

### Season 1990/91

**Tour to Pakistan**

| Venue | Opponents | Runs | Catches |
|---|---|---|---|
| Karachi | Pakistan | 11 | – |

### Season 1991

**Texaco Trophy**

| Venue | Opponents | Runs | Catches |
|---|---|---|---|
| Lord's | England | 23 | – |

### Season 1991/92

**Wills Trophy**

| Venue | Opponents | Runs | Catches |
|---|---|---|---|
| Sharjah | Pakistan | 5 | – |
| Sharjah | India | 45 | – |
| Sharjah | Pakistan | 0 | – |

**Tour to Pakistan**

| Venue | Opponents | Runs | Catches |
|---|---|---|---|
| Karachi | Pakistan | 54 | 1 |
| Lahore | Pakistan | 18 | – |
| Faizalabad | Pakistan | 45 | 2 |

**World Series**

| Venue | Opponents | Runs | Catches |
|---|---|---|---|
| Perth | India | 14 | 2 |
| Melbourne | Australia | 11 | 1 |
| Adelaide | India | 29 | – |
| Sydney | Australia | 19 | – |
| Melbourne | Australia | 22 | – |
| Brisbane | India | 4 | – |
| Brisbane | Australia | 69 | – |
| Melbourne | India | 11 | 1 |

**World Cup**

| Venue | Opponents | Runs | Catches |
|---|---|---|---|
| Melbourne | Pakistan | 88* | – |
| Melbourne | England | 0 | – |
| Brisbane | Zimbabwe | 72 | – |
| Christchurch | S Africa | 9 | 2 |
| Auckland | N Zealand | 52 | – |
| Wellington | India | 41 | – |
| Berri | Sri Lanka | 1 | – |
| Melbourne | Australia | 70 | – |

**South Africa in West Indies**

| Venue | Opponents | Runs | Catches |
|---|---|---|---|
| Kingston | South Africa | 50 | 1 |
| Port–of–Spain | South Africa | 86* | 1 |
| Port–of–Spain | South Africa | 35 | – |

### Season 1992/93

**World Series**

| Venue | Opponents | Runs | Catches |
|---|---|---|---|
| Perth | Pakistan | 59 | 1 |
| Perth | Australia | 29 | – |
| Sydney | Australia | 4 | 1 |
| Adelaide | Pakistan | 15 | – |
| Melbourne | Australia | 74 | – |
| Sydney | Pakistan | 3 | 1 |
| Brisbane | Pakistan | 10 | 3 |
| Brisbane | Australia | 10 | – |
| Sydney | Australia | 67 | 2 |
| Melbourne | Australia | 60 | – |

**West Indies tour to South Africa**

| Venue | Opponents | Runs | Catches |
|---|---|---|---|
| Pt Elizabeth | South Africa | 13 | – |
| Jo'burg | Pakistan | 0 | 1 |
| CapeTown | South Africa | 14 | – |
| Durban | Pakistan | 128 | – |
| Bloemfontein | South Africa | 111* | – |
| Cape Town | Pakistan | 26* | 3 |
| Jo'burg | Pakistan | 49 | – |

**Pakistan in West Indies**

| Venue | Opponents | Runs | Catches |
|---|---|---|---|
| Kingston | Pakistan | 114 | – |
| Port-of-Spain | Pakistan | 95* | – |
| Port-of-Spain | Pakistan | 5 | – |
| St Vincent | Pakistan | 5 | – |
| Georgetown | Pakistan | 15 | – |

### Season 1993/94

**Champions Trophy**

| Venue | Opponents | Runs | Catches |
|---|---|---|---|
| Sharjah | Sri Lanka | 5 | 2 |
| Sharjah | Pakistan | 14 | 3 |
| Sharjah | Pakistan | 14 | 1 |
| Sharjah | Sri Lanka | 42 | – |
| Sharjah | Pakistan | 153 | 1 |

**Hero Cup**

| Venue | Opponents | Runs | Catches |
|---|---|---|---|
| Bombay | Sri Lanka | 67 | – |
| Bombay | South Africa | 7 | 1 |
| Ahmedabad | India | 23 | 2 |
| Hyderabad | Zimbabwe | 4 | 1 |
| Calcutta | Sri Lanka | 82 | 1 |
| Calcutta | India | 33 | – |

**West Indies tour to Sri Lanka**

| Venue | Opponents | Runs | Catches |
|---|---|---|---|
| Colombo | Sri Lanka | 89 | – |
| Colombo | Sri Lanka | 65 | 1 |
| Colombo | Sri Lanka | 29 | – |

**England in West Indies**

| Venue | Opponents | Runs | Catches |
|---|---|---|---|
| Bridgetown | England | 9 | 1 |
| Kingston | England | 8 | – |
| St Vincent | England | 60 | 1 |
| Port-of-Spain | England | 19 | 1 |
| Port-of-Spain | England | 16 | – |

## International average

| Matches | Innings | Not out | Runs | HS | Average | 100s | 50s | Catches |
|---------|---------|---------|------|-----|---------|------|-----|---------|
| 68 | 68 | 5 | 2529 | 153 | 40.14 | 4 | 18 | 39 |

## Playing for Warwickshire

In the Benson & Hedges Cup of 1994, won by Warwickshire, Lara scored 112 runs in 3 innings with a best of 70 against Surrey at The Oval in the semi-final.

Up to 30 July his record in the AXA Sunday League was 147 in 9 matches for an average of 16.33, with a best score of 63 against Kent at Edgbaston.

Up to 30 July Lara had played 2 innings in the 1994 Nat West Trophy competition, scoring 16 against Leicestershire, 9 against Somerset. Warwickshire face Kent in the semi-final.

## PHOTOGRAPH ACKNOWLEDGEMENTS

The author and publishers would like to thank the photographers who supplied pictures for use in this book, as follows:

Shaun Botterill/Allsport page 24 (both pictures)
Gordon Brooks pages 10, 11 (both pictures), 13, 14, 20, 21 (Lara with Desmond Haynes), 26, 36 (Lara with Viv Richards)
Clive Brunskill/Allsport page 60
Chris Cole/Allsport page 21 (Lara at Arundel)
Patrick Eagar pages 2/3 (title spread), 19 (Gus Logie, Roy Fredericks), 56, 61, 67
Express Newspapers pages 44 (detail), 46
Hulton Deutsch Collection pages 19 (Sir Colin Cowdrey), 32
Joe Mann/Allsport pages 23 (Australia v West Indies), 25 (all four pictures)
Adrian Murrell/Allsport pages 23 (West Indies v Pakistan), 27 (second one-day international, Lara bowled by Hick)
News Team International pages 47, 49
Press Association/Barry Batchelor page 54
Ben Radford/Allsport pages 28 (Lara and Jack Russell), 31 (dislodged bail), 37 (Mayfield), 39 (Lara leaving pitch, Lara in the dressing-room), 65 (Lara with Dermot Reeve)
Pascal Rondeau/Allsport page 18

Those pictures not attributed here were all supplied by Graham Morris.